ZOMBIE DAWN
OUTBREAK

MICHAEL G. THOMAS
& NICK S. THOMAS

ISBN 978-1906512637

Typeset by Swordworks Books
Printed and bound in the UK & US
A catalogue record of this book is available from the British Library

Cover design by Swordworks Books
www.swordworks.co.uk

ZOMBIE DAWN
OUTBREAK

CHAPTER ONE

Alaska, United States

Dr Garcia collected her luggage from the small collection area at Wiley Post-Will Rogers Memorial Airport. She'd only been waiting five minutes but that was hardly surprising, the airport served a city of just over four thousand people. It was a small airport for a small city but that didn't make it unimportant. Quite the opposite, this was the home the one of the most advanced federal research sites in the United States. As she left the luggage area she flipped out her mobile phone and called the person that had demanded her presence in this most remote of places. As she lifted the handset to her ear it rang twice until answered. There was no voice at the other end.

"Dr Garcia here, please put me through to Dr Murphy."

There was a succession of clicks and then a series of

rings started. Dr Garcia sighed. The effort of trying to get through to Dr Murphy was always a game she would rather not play. Another series of tones came down the line, it sounded very much like a fax machine or one of those old 8-bit computers with the software on cassettes. She hit the secure button on the phone, followed by her passcode. There were yet more tones until there was a final click and a voice came through.

"Dr Garcia?" asked the voice.

"It's me," answered Dr Garcia.

"Good, have you arrived safely?" asked the man.

She approached the doors of the terminal, barging them open with her bag and stepped out into the bitter weather of Barrow, Alaska.

"Yeah, I'm heading to the car pool. Is the system back online yet?" she asked in a frustrated voice.

As she left the building she stepped out to the road and towards a waiting car, a large black Chrysler 300 limousine. Stood next to the car was a tall man in a black suit and wearing a woollen hat. He spoke quietly to himself and then opened the door. Dr Garcia walked to the car and climbed inside, leaving her case to the man.

"Listen, the situation has got far worse. We've managed to contain the breeches from the first attacks and the firewalls are holding."

"The car's here," she said in matter of fact voice. "I don't like it, wait till I get there. Have you cut the hard lines? You can't afford an external breach, even if the labs are isolated."

"The situation has become far more complicated than that."

"What do you mean?" she asked.

"I can't say on your cell, just come straight to me when you arrive. We have to protect our research data, at any cost."

"Sounds a little ominous Harold! What is so important about it?" asked Dr Garcia.

The car pulled away, the low rumble of the powerful 5.7 litre V8 growling away. As they moved off another identical vehicle pulled out and followed them onto what the locals considered the main road.

Dr Murphy went silent for a moment, then almost whispered down the phone, "Anna, we've had a breakthrough on the project. I mean a real breakthrough."

Dr Garcia considered Dr Murphy's comments for a moment, trying to decide whether this was good or bad news. The fact that she had been called in usually meant the latter. Her curiosity got the better of her.

"As in you've got it to work? No wonder the data connections are under attack. Sounds like you have a mole. Either that or they've been tampered with. The only reason to hit the LSEC system is if somebody has already compromised the labs and is trying to get data out. I assume you have guards at all the LSEC points in the facility?" she said.

"Of course. I can't say any more, you'll be at the centre in a few minutes, come straight to my office, you've got a lot of work today, Doctor."

"I'll be with you shortly," answered Dr Garcia.

She held the phone out and hit the end call button. The possibility that the research centre had made progress was intriguing. She had only the most basic background of what they were working on, but she did know it took up almost the entire research budget. This, and the fact that every major medical research company was itching to get their hands on it, made her just a little uncomfortable. If Dr Murphy was letting it slip that they were getting somewhere then she needed to clamp down on any leaks, and fast.

The small convoy of black cars pulled off the main road and down a much rougher, less used track. Along each side of the road was heaped snow where ploughs had obviously been sometime earlier in the day. Driving in the opposite direction was a black Chevy Blazer, its windows were blacked out and on the doors were the small badges of the Nightguard Security Unit.

The first sign that this wasn't an ordinary centre was the electric fencing and a secure gateway. As the cars approached the gate, two armed guards blocked the road. A third waited inside the gatehouse. These security guards looked almost the same as regular US infantry with their military issue firearms and equipment. What gave them away though was the insignia dotted over their clothing, the markings of the Nightguard private security company. Since the explosion in recruitment for private military contractors in Iraq many of these companies had started up. Nightguard specialised in installation protection and was now one of the most powerful security firms in the United States. The vehicles stopped at the gateway whilst one of the guards approached the driver's window. The driver lowered the window and handed over his pass. The guard scanned it, a high-pitched beep coming from his scanner. He then moved to the rear doors and tapped on the glass.

Dr Garcia pressed the button on the door and the window slid smoothly down.

"Dr Garcia?" asked the guard.

"Yes," she answered as she handed him her plastic security pass.

The man examined it for a moment as he scanned it. Dr Garcia could make out scrolling text and images from his security tablet in the reflection of his mirrored sunglasses. The guard then walked over to the gate and spoke to the man inside. There was a pause for another ten seconds and then he returned.

"We are on a Level Red Lockdown, Doctor. Your vehicles are the last to be allowed on site. A security detail will escort you from the entrance," he said.

Dr Garcia nodded in acknowledgement as the guard handed back her pass. It was a small biometric security card with her picture, barcode, name and security chip on it. The guard stepped back and the gate started to lift up. The two cars moved through the gateway and approached the main building. It was distinctly uninspiring to the untrained eye. From the front it looked like a single storey building with a glass entrance and a helipad on its roof. There were no guards actually outside the building, but Dr Garcia knew from her last visit that there was no shortage of people inside. In front of the building was a small parking lot with just three other vehicles parked. The only other structure of note was a large mast that was attached to the side of the building. There were multiple microwave transmitters dotted up the structure and several dishes pointing high into the sky. The top of the tower contained a final antenna, probably added another twenty feet to the metal construction. She was reminded of a local public access TV station as the car pulled in front of the building.

The front doors opened and two heavily armed security guards approached her car, one opening the door, the second watching the area for trouble. As Dr Garcia exited the vehicle she noticed scorch marks on the walls near the door and what looked like bullet marks nearby. Her first thoughts were that it looked like the facility had been attacked. The doors opened to reveal a small room that led to a second set of doors. She moved forward, the guards flanking her on each side. The outer doors slid shut and almost at the same time the inner doors slid open to reveal the foyer. What greeted her confirmed her worst fears. There were scorch marks on the floor and the glass entrance to the elevator in the centre of the room was cracked and damaged. Around the sides of the room were security terminals and half a dozen guards. Two of the desks were badly damaged and several technicians were repairing systems off to the right. As the inner doors slid shut a short, stocky man in body armour and carrying a rifle on his shoulder approached.

"Dr Garcia, I'm Security Chief Allen. I'm to escort you to Dr Murphy," he said in a matter of fact tone.

She nodded, following the man to the elevator. Though the glass was cracked and damaged the security console was still operational. The Security Chief scanned his own card and Dr Garcia did the same. The inner tube opened so that they could enter. The scanners beeped as each entered the elevator. The guard hit a button on the panel and it started a quick and very smooth descent.

"When were you attacked?" asked Dr Garcia.

"About seven hours ago. I wasn't here when it happened though. You'll need to get the details from Dr Murphy," came his curt reply.

Dr Garcia raised her eyebrows, "I see."

The elevator slowed and then stopped, the doors

sliding open into a long corridor. The guard stayed inside, gesturing down the corridor.

"You know the way?" he asked.

Dr Garcia nodded and left, heading directly down the corridor. As she reached the door at the end she heard the elevator returning to the surface above her. Like all the doors in this facility, it was security locked and encoded. Once again she needed to swipe her access card, enter her code and also provide a thumb scan before the green light flashed. With a hiss the door opened to reveal a large computer centre. In the centre of the room was a massive display, probably ten feet tall and around it were clusters of terminals, smaller displays and about a dozen people, all in lab coats working away. A man approached her, it was Dr Murphy. He held out his hand, shaking hers firmly.

"I'm glad to see you here Anna, we need your help," he said in an almost pleading voice.

He turned and walked towards the large screen, she followed.

"What happened?" she asked.

"Forty-eight hours ago the experiment reached its first successful test. Within an hour of the data being secured we were hit by a series of computer hacks on the main network, specifically against our firewalls," he explained.

"But all the labs are independent of the network though. Even if somebody breaches the outer firewalls, they can only get access to the public network," she said.

Dr Murphy pointed up to the screen where it showed a detail schematic of the research centre. He pointed to several points out on the perimeter of the building.

"Of course. Plus they can only access the secure internal network if they actually gain physical access to one of the three data points within this centre. The problem is that somebody managed to get inside," he said.

"What!" she shouted, "How?"

"One of the analysts managed to copy part of the test data and tried to get out of the building with it. It looks like at least two other personnel were helping him. They managed to get to the foyer but were intercepted by one of our security teams."

"Intercepted? Is that a euphemism for shooting them? I saw the damage upstairs."

"That damage isn't from the escape attempt. It's from the team that came in right after him. If they'd arrived sixty seconds earlier they would have escaped with them," he added.

Dr Murphy pointed at the foyer on the screen. He tapped it, zooming out to show the facility and the surrounding area.

"The group of three were stopped from leaving the foyer by the door security team. There were no casualties though until an ambulance bluffed its way through the outer gate," he pointed at the entrance, "and deployed an armed team around the entrance of the compound."

He tapped the screen and the large display split up into a dozen different security camera feeds. Dr Murphy pointed out the most significant ones, specifically an external feed at the entrance and a wide angle shot of the foyer. The team from the ambulance moved to the doors and placed something on the frame. There was a flash and the external feed was shrouded in white smoke. On the interior camera a group of men in black rushed in to engage in a firefight with the security staff. The scene became a mess until the doctor paused the action, pointing directly at the bottom left corner.

"See that?" he asked.

Dr Garcia stepped closer, examining the screen carefully, "It looks like one of them is carrying a specimen case."

Dr Murphy hit the screen and the action commenced. Both of them continued watching but concentrated on the man with the case. There were more flashes from weapons and the then the person moved back, towards the elevator, grabbing somebody else in a lab coat. In just a few seconds they disappeared back below. In the foyer another security team had arrived and in just a few more shots the battle was over.

Dr Murphy turned back to Dr Garcia.

"This is the problem. The data analyst has not just stolen a vast amount of classified data, he's also taken one of our top researchers, Dr Morovitz. He managed to break into the data centre and barricaded himself inside," he said.

"The data centre? Does he have access to the secure servers?" asked Dr Garcia.

"Not just that, he's already cut the data lines and is threatening to set off a bomb at the core if we don't give him access to an external data line. If he does that we'll lose the data, the samples, and Dr Morovitz. That would be the end of the project and the end of this centre."

"Does he know what the project is and what does he have in the case?" asked Dr Garcia.

"Yes it seems so, but that isn't the biggest problem of all. He has the only viable sample of the Tetrodotoxin-A solution," said Dr Murphy.

One of the technicians rushed over to the doctor, interrupting their conversation.

"He's on the intercom," said the man.

Dr Murphy moved up to a desk that faced the large screen, beckoning Garcia to come with him. He sat down and hit the intercom connect button.

"Dr Murphy here. Is Morovitz okay?" he asked.

"For now," came a menacing voice back on the system.

"You have ten minutes to provide me with four clean high speed ports with unrestricted access through the firewalls. If I do not have access in ten minutes I'll destroy this room, your precious doctor and the sample," he demanded.

Dr Garcia was already speeding through the security protocols on the terminal next to Dr Murphy. She locked out any possible pathways from the room to any other part of the facility.

"You know we can't do that, your actions are sabotage against a Federal facility," said Dr Murphy.

"I know what you've been doing here. Either you give us what we want or you'll pay the price!" he screamed.

Dr Garcia checked the communication system, making sure it was muted before she spoke. She leaned towards Dr Murphy.

"Do you have a security team down there?" whispered Dr Garcia.

Dr Murphy looked at her then double-checked on his screen.

"Yes, we have a six man tactical unit as well as a full decontaminant team."

Dr Murphy hit a few keys, loading up a display that showed the blocked room as well as the security team that were waiting in position. The room was sealed and surrounded. There was no way the man was getting out alive, unless they deemed it necessary.

"What can you tell me about the project? Why is he so desperate to get access to it?" she asked.

"You know I can't tell you that, all you need to know is that it is biological and if data relating to it is leaked, it will be a major national security breach."

"So, you're feeding me the usual research project bullshit then?" she said sarcastically.

"Well, in that case, I don't think you have many choices. We can try and fake the connections but we have no way of knowing what he is expecting. I suggest we use the emergency protocols to end the situation quickly," she added.

"You mean the internal defence system? If we use it we'll kill him and Dr Morovitz," he retorted.

"If you don't you'll lose them both as well as the sample and the data," she said coldly.

"If you want to preserve the sample and data you need to release the nerve agent and fast, before he does something irreversible," she continued.

Dr Garcia scanned through the security screens, checking that all the defensive systems were still operational. Several windows popped up signalling that some of the systems were off-line. She ran several emergency scripts that brought three of them back up.

"They're taking out the security systems, I think somebody else is accessing the security net," said Garcia as she looked around the room.

"I recommend immediate action if you want to stay in control of the situation," continued Garcia.

Dr Murphy, a computing specialist in his own right, turned back to his terminal accessing several high security subroutines that only he and the high level staff had access to.

"I think I can get access to the internal video feed if I reconfigure the climate control ports to retransmit the cameras. Give me a second," he said.

As Dr Murphy continued on the video feed Dr Garcia hammered away at the keyboard to try and protect the sensitive firewalls and routers. She rewrote the port forwarding and decryption control scripts and within a few more seconds the firewalls were locked down and the data appeared safe.

"Can you give me a hand with this?" asked Dr Murphy as he transferred his screen over to Garcia.

The access screens popped up on her terminal, as well as the climate control and video control servers. In just thirty seconds she had removed the control of part of the air circulation system and piggybacked the video stream. The large screen in the centre of the room flashed and then displayed a hazy image of the room where the doctor was being held.

"Fuck me!" shouted one of the technicians as he saw the plight of their top researcher.

To their horror they could see the doctor was tied and gagged in the corner of the room, and with what looked like bloody wounds on his face. Dr Garcia moved up to the screen, examining the room's layout.

"It looks like he's rigged the door with something,

look," she said.

On the door there appeared to be a rectangular device, it was placed to the side of the door frame and had the ominous look of a bomb of some kind.

"If he's rigged the room we're going to have to use the internal countermeasures," said Dr Garcia.

She returned to the computer console.

"I'm going to ready the system, it will be ready in about twenty seconds."

Dr Murphy stood silent, weighing up the options. The internal countermeasures were designed to protect the sensitive site against terrorist attacks. It was a two stage system to first eliminate any hostile biological threat, including the terrorists themselves, and second to stop any fires or similar attempts to destroy equipment.

To facilitate this response a combination of short life nerve gas and nitrogen was pumped in. The nerve gas killed almost instantly but lost viability in just seconds. This meant the room could be safely reoccupied after a few minutes. The second part of the system pumped in a large volume of inert nitrogen. This would starve fire of oxygen and protect valuable technology and equipment from fire or explosives that were still burning.

"Ok, get it ready and standby. If we can't get the doctor out safely then we will have to neutralise the threat," he said.

The intercom crackled and the voice of the man

returned.

"Time's up, where's my data line?"

"We're having problems getting it resolved because of the damage from the attack. We'll have it working in about an hour," answered Dr Murphy.

"Bullshit!" shouted the man.

On the screen the man could be seen walking towards the tied up doctor. He moved up close and then held the wireless intercom near the man's face. He placed it down on the floor and then pulled out a hand gun and pointed it directly at the man's face. He continued shouting down the line.

"Don't fuck with me. I know you can connect me in seconds and I also know you're monitoring this room. This is what happens if you treat me like this!" he screamed.

He lowered the pistol and fired a single shot into the doctor's leg. The detail wasn't perfect on the large screen but it was good enough to show the red blood on the floor and to see the doctor writhing in pain. The man continued shouting at the intercom.

"You have thirty seconds or I'll blow the shit out of this place, thirty seconds!" he shouted.

Dr Murphy turned to Dr Garcia.

"We have to stop him. If that sample gets out into the open and the integrity of the room is breached we could have a major incident here. I'm talking major," he said.

"Couldn't you have told me this earlier?" said an

irritated Dr Garcia.

"Like I said, it's a need to know business. Are you ready?"

The hostage taker had now lifted up the sample case and was hitting the locking mechanism with the pistol. He shouted into the intercom.

"Five seconds and I blow us all to shit!" he screamed.

"Now!" shouted Dr Murphy as he turned back to Garcia, "Hit it!"

Dr Garcia looked at the screen one more time. There was nothing that could be done. It was either kill the two men in the room or half the facility would be destroyed, plus the two men, the sample, the data and a potential major biochemical incident.

She hit the run button on the touch screen and triggered the automated security system, it would take just seconds. She watched the large view screen carefully. A tone emitted from the terminal, indicating the start of the sequence.

The man held up the now damaged case in one hand and in his right the pistol. Throwing it down he held out a trigger type device, and then it happened. The tone from the terminal changed, it was the nerve gas and the effect was instant. The man shuddered on the screen and then collapsed to the floor. Without even a glimpse of movement it appeared he was dead before he hit the ground. The wriggling doctor in the corner of the room had stopped moving though the pool of blood near his wounded leg continued to grow.

One of the technicians shouted out, now only spotting the deaths of the two men. Another vomited over his terminal. Back on the screen there was no sign of movement. Dr Garcia stood up and walked over to Dr Murphy.

"This is bad. The fact that this facility was breached is one thing, the fact that one of your staff was able to get this far is inexcusable. I'm going to need to interview everybody that was here. We need to stay in lockdown until this situation is resolved. Also, what about the data, is it still intact?"

Dr Murphy was shell-shocked. He just sat there in his chair starring at the screen.

"I've known him for thirteen years, we've been working on this project for half of that time," he muttered.

The door opened and in walked three of the armed guards. The largest of the group spoke first.

"Sir, we've found three more devices and have disabled them," he said.

Dr Garcia stepped in.

"Devices, as in explosives?" she asked.

The guard looked at Dr Murphy first who then nodded, giving him the confirmation he needed.

"Yes, they aren't armed, luckily they must have rushed planting them. They're C4 based but the triggers were all remote. We isolated the signal and set up a block whilst we removed the detonators. The problem though is that we have traced the signal and it looks like there could be up to three more in the facility."

"This looks like a major operation to me. You need to get a Federal response cleared while we locate the rest of the charges," said Garcia.

"What the hell!" shouted one of the technicians who stood in front of the large screen. It was still broadcasting the feed from the room.

Dr Garcia looked before realising that the doctor was standing up whilst the hostage taker was up on one leg. She rushed to her terminal, checked the screen for the progress of the internal security system.

"I don't understand, the room has been flooded. Nothing can live in that room."

"No, no!" shouted Dr Murphy as he pointed at the floor, "Look!"

On the screen the sample case was clearly damaged and something was leaking out onto the floor. One of the men was staggering towards the booby trapped door, seemingly oblivious to the explosives attached to it. Dr Murphy turned to the pillar nearby and hit a large red button. Red lights started flashing around the room and a low level klaxon started its drone. He pressed the button and hit the intercom.

"This is a Level One Containment Breach. This is not

a drill. All rooms are being sealed, no personnel are to enter or leave the facility. Tactical teams are to follow protocols," he said.

He hit the button on the intercom that repeated his message continually. Dr Garcia triggered the internal system one more, flooding the room with the lethal concoction of gasses.

The screen went black and immediately the facility shook from the impact of an explosion deep inside the centre. The sound followed a dull crump. Dr Garcia hit a key, scanning through available security cameras until she reached the one in the corridor outside the room. The screen was initially full of white smoke but as it started to clear the scene became one of devastation and blood. The blast had destroyed the doorway and part of the wall. Blood and gore were plastered on the corridor from either the hostage taker or from the security personnel that had been waiting on the other side for the order to breach. She moved the small control joystick, moving the camera to examine the rest of the hallway.

About twenty feet from the door were the bodies of half a dozen heavily armoured security personnel. They were not moving though whether this was from the blast or the nerve gas wasn't obvious. Part of the corridor on the opposite side from the blown door was damaged, leaving several jagged holes the size of dustbin lids in the wall. She turned to look in the opposite direction towards to elevator. The entire glass side of it was smashed and the bloodied bodies of two technicians lay on the floor, presumably killed by the gas and injured by the glass.

Dr Murphy slumped in his chair, shaking his head. Dr Garcia stood up and after taking in a deep breath, reverted to her role as the company's trouble-shooter.

"I'll take over from here. We need anybody affected by the chemicals to be put into quarantine. I'll take a biohazard team down to investigate," she said.

Dr Murphy, still in shock simply nodded. Garcia left the room, flanked by two of the armed guards and headed to the closest containment room where the Hazmat suits and equipment were held. She was obviously well versed in using the equipment as in less than a minute she was fully dressed in an enclosed biohazard suit and making her way to the emergency access staircase. Waiting for her there were four members of the security staff, each wearing the same suits. The only major difference being that each man was carrying a SCAR modular rifle. These futuristic looking weapons were made by Fabrique Nationale de Herstal for the U.S. Special Operations Command. The weapon was the SCAR-L variant, chambered the 5.56x45mm NATO cartridge and perfect for use by military contractors.

"Ready?" she asked.

The four men nodded, locking their weapons. Dr Garcia led the unit down the staircase to the east access point where they waited behind the door. The smoke, dust and chemicals hadn't been able to penetrate the two sealed doors from the staircase into the corridor. Dr Garcia held out her arm, attached to her suit was a sophisticated looking bio analysis tool. It displayed a sequence of colours and figures describing the environment. After tapping a few buttons she was satisfied that the area was clear and gave the men the nod.

The first man hit a button on the door that slid it open to the side. The scanner picked up nothing untoward through the first airlock so the group entered and closed the door behind them. Once again Dr Garcia double-checked the area, still clear. With a final nod the door opened and the four men burst in, taking up defensive positions around the entrance.

More smoke flooded the corridor as the airflow patterns changed with the opening door. As the dust cleared the guards were shocked to find no bodies on the floor where they had been on the view screens. One of the guards cried out, falling to the ground with two badly injured technicians on top of him. As the guards turned they could see more of the wounded coming towards them. They moved with a bizarre slowness as though they were in the throes of rigamortis as they stepped.

"Fuck me!" shouted the guard to her left as he fumbled with his firearm.

Two of the guards moved in, smashing their rifle butts into the heads of the wounded people. It was bloody work but after several heavy swipes they had reached the injured man. They dragged him back towards the doorway.

Dr Garcia called in on her intercom, "We've got a serious problem down here. Something has happened to those exposed. I don't know if it's from the security system, or from your sample."

"What if somebody tampered with the system, maybe pumped something else in to interfere with the research?" asked one of the guards.

Dr Garcia considered his comments for a moment before speaking back into her intercom.

"I suggest we..." she was interrupted before she could finish.

From out of the dust another group of the injured had appeared and this time they were striking with their arms and hands at the group. Though the guards beat them back there was something inhuman about their eyes and movement. As the close quarter fighting continued Dr Garcia bent down to examine the wounded man. His face appeared pale through the protective transparent screen over his head. She was about to touch him with her hand when he started to shake and spasm, classic symptoms of a deadly biological attack of some kind.

The door opened and another four men in Hazmat suits rushed in, two held him down whilst the other two moved into the corridor to help their beleaguered comrades.

Dr Garcia stepped back, keeping away from the trouble

whilst she continued her dialogue with Dr Murphy.

"The situation is dangerous down here. It's getting out of control. I think we have some kind of psycho traumatic outbreak that has affected the people down here."

"Can you reach the damaged sample?" came back the voice on the headset.

Dr Garcia turned to the left and looked down at the damage in the corridor where the explosion had occurred.

"I'll take a look," she said.

She took several steps, moving past the wounded man on the ground as he was being held down. The fighting continued ahead as the guards pushed back the wounded or more likely, the infected. She stopped as one of the guards was overwhelmed and knocked to the floor. Another of the infected victims fell down onto him, clawing at his weapon. The man on the ground must have panicked because a long burst of gunfire poured from his Skar rifle, tearing apart the man trying to attack him. The injured man stumbled back several feet, multiple bullet holes in his chest. Dark blood sprayed against the already scorched walls. He staggered a little more and then stopped. Shaking his arm he proceeded towards the man with the weapon.

"Stun them!" shouted the leader of the tactical guards.

One of the men took out a stun grenade from his belt and pulled the pin. These grenades were special versions, based upon the standard military and police issue items.

They were designed with a tiny, non damaging blast radius but could incapacitate enemies at a distance for several minutes. As he moved his hand to throw the weapon another of the infected threw himself at the guard, knocking him back. The grenade fell from his hand, hitting the ground and then bouncing. The guard leapt for the grenade but it was too late. With three quick beeps the device armed itself and then detonated. In the narrow confines of the corridor the effect was devastating. The initial blast, though small, was enough to burn through one the of Hazmat suits. The concussive blast though knocked all of them within five metres to the ground. Though it was designed to stun or incapacitate people it was not intended to be dropped into a group as densely populated as this.

Dr Garcia was stunned by the blast and thrown hard against the wall. The emergency klaxon had kicked in again, adding its monotonous drone to the sounds of movement and people. As she slid to the floor the sound became muffled and dull as the concussion took hold. In just seconds she passed out, the sounds fading until they became nothing at all.

The darkness faded away and light returned to her eyes slowly. It could have been seconds, minutes or even hours, she had no idea. She tried to focus, seeing people and movement off into the distance. Her throat was sore, she badly needed a drink. She tried to move but something was holding her down. She tried to focus, hearing voices and shouting.

Then came the gun shots.

CHAPTER TWO

Queensland, Australia
9:00am

Bruce was stumbling out of his Burgundian tent, it had been a heavy night. It was the second day of the medieval re-enactment event. Aching from the day before, and having had rather a large quantity of beer in the night, he stumbled over to a nearby tree to relieve himself, only to notice the organiser's wife being in plain view. He didn't care.

It was already fully light and the day was warming up quickly, another sweatfest. Bruce had been re-enacting for over ten years now, it provided a great outlet from his job as a PR consultant. In his job he had to be painfully nice to everyone, when he'd only want to hammer them on the head with a poleaxe, so this hobby suited him well.

Bruce was a married man, though you would rarely know it, his wife spending so much time with her family in England. But this always provided a lot of time for his hobbies, especially as she always took the kids with her. He stumbled several hundred yards over to the toilet block, a luxury he wasn't always afforded, though this event took place at the local rugby and football club.

Getting to the basin he threw a cupped hand full of water onto his face. The sharp cool shock was a pleasant wake up from the dazed state he was in. He looked up at himself in the mirror. Water dripped from his short beard onto the dirty arming jacket he'd not bothered to remove in the night. The quilted garment was near white when it began life, but was now a greasy and dirty stained mix of black and cream, the result of regular contact with mail armour.

He wandered back to the line of historical tents. Bruce's closest friends, Dylan and Connor, were sat around a gas stove cooking bacon for brekkie. It was an unavoidable smell for him to pass up, sizzling meat after a beer fuelled night and dehydrated morning.

"Got any going spare?" asked Bruce.

He knew his mates would always have some going for him, but he never liked to make them feel he treated them as slaves, or that he was a bludger, which in many ways he was.

"Of course mate, sit down," said Dylan.

With bacon in the belly and the sun shining down, the day was quickly firing up, one more day of fun before it was back to the grindstone. By ten o'clock the three had done little to move from their comfortable position. They all knew that the crowds would be flocking in anytime now, but none could be bothered to put any effort in.

"You know we have a battle at eleven, yeh?" said Connor.

"Yeh, suppose it's about time to armour up," said Bruce.

"Our numbers are a bit low today aren't they?" asked Dylan.

"A few people were sick on Friday and cancelled, a couple of others went home last night as they were rough," said Connor.

"Great, the organiser won't be happy, I'd be amazed if we can field more than twenty combatants, not exactly an epic battle," said Bruce.

"Fuck 'em, the public suck anyway," said Dylan.

"Well then you should've joined the SCA!" said Bruce.

Dylan didn't respond, just huffed at the response. The group was due to put on a battle re-enactment display shortly, and they were yet to even put away their modern cooker. Finally the three got up and went to work.

Bruce went about fitting his armour, a tricky job without help. He tied up the arming jacket that he was still wearing and sat down with the bag of armour. He started with the cuisses, poleyns and greaves, the leg armour. He then threw over his mail shirt, wriggling to get it to tumble over his body. It was another half an hour before he finally had attached the mail gorget, plate arms and breastplate. It was now just ten minutes until the display and the group was finally approaching a ready state, a lazy display of organisation.

"Come on you bogan bastard!" shouted Connor.

Bruce stood up in a relaxed lazy fashion, unaffected by his friend's attempts to hurry him along, and happy to continue at the pace he intended. He pulled his gauntlets on and took his poleaxe in hand, but before he began to make a move, Bruce noticed a ruckus forming a hundred yards away where the public had been wandering around the local fair. Taking a few steps closer he could hear the cries of a woman asking for a doctor. He leapt forwards, breaking away from his usual casual and lazy state, for one showing determination.

Breaking through the crowd of people Bruce could see the cause of the problem. A boy was lying on the floor, his father crouched over him. The lad of about eight years old was very pale and sickly, barely able to breathe.

"Are you a doctor?" the mother asked.

"No, but I can help," said Bruce.

He knelt down beside the boy. The young lad was perspiring heavily, clearly in a feverish state. His breathing had slowed to a feint gasp.

"Have you called an ambulance?" Bruce asked.

"Yes, but it won't be here for another five minutes, please help him!" the mother said.

The boy coughed harshly and blood splurged out from his mouth.

"What's his name?" asked Bruce.

"John," the father responded.

"Ok John, can you hear me?" asked Bruce.

The boy let out his final breath. The audience around him gasped in horror as they saw the boy lose all signs of life.

"He's stopped breathing, you give mouth to mouth, I'll give the compressions," said Bruce to the boy's father.

The man, in utter panic, began breathing air into his son's mouth. Bruce began the compressions. The two men cycled the same action again. As Bruce was pushing down on the boy's heart, he jolted and spluttered.

"Out the way!" said Bruce.

He laid his ear down close to the boy's head to listen for breathing. He listened intently whilst the crowd was silent around him. The boy's body jerked up and he bit into Bruce's collar. He leapt to his feet, the boy still clinging on with his jaw.

"What the fuck!" Bruce shouted.

The boy's teeth stood no chance of penetrating Bruce's mail collar, a fact he would truly learn to appreciate before the day was out. He circled around, trying to pull the crazy boy from him.

"Get this bloody bastard off me!" Bruce cried.

The boy's father took hold of the boy as his mother was shrieking in amazement and horror. The boy released his hold on Bruce, who was thrown to the ground from the sudden balance change. The crazy boy simply did the same to his father as he had attempted with Bruce. This time the child's jaws were rather more successful, driving hard into the man's neck, piercing his windpipe. The man collapsed to the ground immediately, his hands cupping the gaping wound, but it was too late. A quickly expanding pool of blood was gathering from around his writhing body.

"Wayne!" shouted the mother.

She ran to his side, but he couldn't respond with anything more than a deathly stare as he gasped for air. She shot a look of disgust at her son, no longer showing any signs of concern for him.

"What have you done?" she cried.

The crowd could do nothing but stare in utter amazement at the situation. The boy staggered towards his parents, blood pouring from his mouth.

"Stay away from us!" she shouted.

He didn't stop. The mother put her right arm out to stop the boy, but he simply took hold and bit into the exposed flesh. The mother reeled in pain. Before Bruce could respond, the boy had driven his teeth in to the woman's neck, the same way he had her husband. Seeing the dire situation before him, Bruce slipped his steel gauntlets back on, full well appreciating what good his armour had already done him.

As the woman tumbled to the ground, Bruce grabbed the boy by his shoulders and threw him aside, away from the woman. He looked down at the bleeding mother and realised she was done for. Bruce looked back at the boy he'd thrown to the ground, the frenzied lad was already back on his feet and stumbling towards Bruce. Now without hesitation, he stood and drove his plate metal gauntlet in to the youngster's face. The sharp edged metal finger sections of the glove drove through the boy's soft skulled head, imbedding a couple of inches in. The result was nothing short of a car crash effect. Putting his other hand onto the boy's lifeless body, he drew the blood soaked gauntlet from his face.

Without warning, Bruce was struck across the head with a baseball bat. One of the nearby stall holders had rushed to the scene to see three dead bodies and a blood soaked man, and rushed to the obvious conclusion.

Bruce came back to consciousness ten minutes later. He was lying flat out, his two friends looking down on him. Water dripped from his face, an attempt by his friends to wake him up. Blood dripped from his head from the strike he'd taken. Looking around, he was in the toilet block that he'd been in earlier in the morning.

"Hey mate, he's back!" said Connor.

"Bruce, Bruce! Come on, mate," said Dylan.

Bruce turned and got to his feet with help from his two friends, still feeling a little unsteady, he rested back against a sink.

"What the fuck is going on?" asked Bruce.

"You tell us,mate," said Dylan.

Looking around, Bruce could see that the door to the toilet room was shut and that two other people were in there with the three friends. One was another re-enactor, Christian, a fairly new member to the group. The other man was a member of the public.

"What are we doing in here?" asked Bruce.

"When you were knocked out everything went to shit," said Connor.

"That couple came back to life and started biting people," said Dylan.

"What do you mean came back to life?" asked Bruce.

"Exactly that, mate. They bled out, and then a minute later were on their feet," said Dylan.

Bruce shook his head in astonishment, lost for words. He turned around to look at himself in the mirror, now more a mess than he was during his last visit.

"What do we do now?" asked Connor.

"Well what's happening out there?" asked Bruce.

"Those people that died and came back, they're wandering around and biting more people, that's why we are held up here," said Dylan.

Bruce stumbled over to a small high window to look out at the carnage. A few dozen of these walking dead were clearly visible, staggering around before him. A line of cars from the entrance to the place was banked up. Several had crashed into one another at the gates, blocking the rest. The walking dead were attacking the people stuck in cars. Some people were getting out and making a run for it.

"Holy dooley!" said Bruce.

"What are they?" asked Connor.

"Look like zombies to me, mate," said Dylan.

"What?" asked Bruce.

"They come back from the dead and bite people, who then become like them. If something acts and looks like a zombie, I call it one," said Dylan.

"Fair dinkum," said Connor.

"Pig's arse!" said Bruce.

"Seems like it, mate," said Dylan.

"Christ, this is bollocks," said Bruce.

"So we're gonna get out of here?" said Connor.

"Bet your arse we are," said Bruce.

He looked around to the car park, his beloved UTE sat peacefully and untouched.

"We need our weapons, we'll cark it without them," said Bruce.

"Yeh," said Connor.

"So, these crazy fuckers are slower than us. We'll make

a run for the tents, grab the weapons, then to the UTE and away," said Bruce.

"How do we get out? The exit is fucked," said Connor.

"Don't you worry about that mate, we'll find a way," said Bruce.

"Right," said Connor.

"Now, who's this?" said Bruce, looking at the only man not suitably attired in armour.

The man looked up, scared and in shock. He was in his early twenties and casually dressed.

"Come on man, speak up," said Bruce.

"Lee," the man reservedly replied.

"Right, Lee. You can either grow some balls, and follow us, or have them removed by Zombies. Which is it going to be?" asked Bruce.

"Uhhh, I'll, uhh, go with you I guess," said Lee.

Bruce slapped the young man, though forgetting he was still wearing steel gauntlets, the hit landed harder than he anticipated, throwing the man off his feet.

"Harden the fuck up, or those things will bleed you dryer than a dead dingo's donger," said Bruce.

Connor and Dylan helped the man back to his feet, the shock had at least woken him up.

"It's alright laddie, he's got your best interests at heart," said Dylan.

"Christian, you with us?" said Bruce.

"Sure thing, boss," said Christian.

Bruce wasn't anyone's boss, but he'd shown some serious initiative so far, whilst most others were panicking or crying like girls. Christian full well knew the best option when he saw it.

"Good, right, how do we kill these fuckers?" asked Bruce.

"You punching its face in seemed to work well," said Dylan.

"Yeh, like in Shaun of the Dead mate, hit them on the head," said Connor.

"Alright, we need our weapons," said Bruce.

"But they're blunt mate," said Connor.

"And? I think a blunt metal poleaxe will hit rather harder than Shaun's cricket bat," said Bruce.

"Too right!" said Dylan.

Bruce looked back out through the window. There were now a dozen zombies shambling between the toilet block and tents. The disease had spread at an incredible rate.

Simply put, too many people were unable to accept the possibility of a zombie apocalypse, and were too shocked to fight back. Many of the others were subdued when the bingle with the speeding ambulance at the entrance blocked most people in.

"Okay, so you ready?" asked Bruce.

The men all nodded. Dylan and Connor were raring to go, Christian uneasy, but comforted by his leader. Lee was still cowering like a little girl. He would clearly follow wherever the survivors went, but Bruce knew he served no useful purpose, except perhaps to provide some diversion.

"Connor, get the door, all of you, follow me, only fight if you have to and keep up!" said Bruce.

He pulled the door open. The heavy clang of the metal door alerted several nearby beasts to their presence, turning to confront the new enemies. The group ran out from the toilets, Bruce at the lead. He zigzagged between the first few. The slow speed of the creatures allowed the men to pass comfortably between them.

Some people would have you believe that armour makes you sluggish and clumsy. The reality is that decent armour weighs a lot less than what a modern soldier carries on his back alone. Well fitted armour moves in near harmony with the body. The weight is divided quite evenly across the body. Armour of course slows your movement by shear weight, and the under armour insulates you heavily. You will indeed sweat more and tire more quickly, but the effects are not near as prominent as most people think. It's not wearing armour that truly tires you, it's fighting which tires you more quickly than many realise, whether you are wearing a full harness or not.

Now just ten feet from his tent, Bruce couldn't avoid walking within grabbing distance of a zombie. Without stopping, he smashed it with a right hook as he ran past. The beast spun around from the almighty force, crashing over a canvas tent before slumping ungraciously to the ground.

The group reached Bruce's tent. He kept a wooden rack for weapons outside his tent for himself and his friends to make use of. He was keen to practice from historical fighting manuals when he could. He reached for his poleaxe and turned to the others. The weapon had an aluminium head on it, making for a safer weapon when using high contact levels against fellow re-enactors. It only made the weapon safer for armoured opponents, not the rest of the population.

The poleaxe was a pole weapon as tall as a man, with a metal axe or hammer head one side, and a spike the other, as well as a top spike. This weapon could more accurately be described as a pole hammer, but the term poleaxe had come in to such regular usage that few people ever differentiated between them anymore.

Connor snatched up his all metal flanged mace, a brutally simple and effective tool. Dylan took up his bardiche, also blunt, but it was a hefty lump of metal. Bruce gave a bill to Christian and Lee. The bill, or billhook, was essentially a long hafted weapon with big steel blade at one end, with spikes and weight in its favour. Christian was capable enough but Lee looked like a complete arse, an incapable and a weak excuse for a man.

Bruce looked around in all directions to evaluate the new situation. Their speedy movement had alerted dozens of creatures to their presence. Clearly, the majority of the crowd that had gathered to watch their display had succumbed to the beasts, at least those that could not flee in time.

The event organiser and his wife, now zombies, were closest. Dylan took note of this and moved towards them with his bardiche. The weapon resembled a long shafted axe but with an elongated semi-circular blade running the last quarter of the shaft. The original weapon would have provided immense cutting ability, but Dylan's re-enactment one was blunt and simply a big cudgel when used in anger.

Dylan swung the weapon around with a shorthanded grip, making full use of the pendulum of steel he wielded. The blunt blade barely noticed the barrier in its path that was the organiser's jaw. The mouth tore open, splitting partly from the upper skull. The zombie's body barrelled over to the ground, though was not dead. It writhed on the floor, not in agony, but desperation. It was not concerned about death, only the endless devotion to drawing more blood.

"Dylan!" shouted Connor.

The second zombie, previously the organiser's wife, was within feet of Dylan, staggering eagerly forwards. Dylan had stopped out of curiosity to see the result of his work, forgetting the world around him. Connor leapt forward and hammered the mace down on to the woman's head. The flanges of the mace imbedded deeply into her brain, so far that the shaft now touched the skull. The zombie dropped to its knees, but the weapon was still firmly rooted in the caved in noggin.

"Corker of a shot!" shouted Bruce.

He could barely conceal his excitement. Just a few hours before he almost felt bad about urinating in the presence of the woman, now he was not even bothered by her brutal death. A warmth overcame our hero and rid him of the few inhibitions he had left, now he had a real purpose in life.

He looked around to see Lee, quivering in fear and disgust. The coward dropped his weapon and chundered next to Bruce's tent. Bruce's moment of awesomeness was over, time to put the game face back on. He strode over to the pathetic man, fully aware of the evil that was bearing down on the group.

"You pathetic, lazy, idle, fuck muppet! You're about as useful as a one-legged man in an arse kicking contest!" said Bruce.

The man looked up at him, gaining some semblance of a man's constitution.

"Bruce?" asked Connor.

"What?" asked Bruce.

"We've got a shit storm bearing down on us, mate!" said Connor.

"Lee, you can either come or stay, I don't give a fuck, but God help you if you slow us down!"

He looked to survey the situation for the last time before they moved. It was truly incredible how quickly the infection had spread. For a moment Bruce wondered how it had even got to this place. Knowing that it was a public re-enactment, where people both locals and outsiders all gathered in one place, he'd already answered his own query.

"To the car!" said Bruce.

The group took to a jogging pace. It was about four hundred yards to the car, they couldn't risk excessively tiring themselves, nor did the enemy's slow speed necessitate them going any faster. Four zombies were mingling in front of Bruce's car up ahead. They had to be dealt with.

"Dylan, go left, Connor right, Christian, you're with me, Lee, stay the fuck out the way!" said Bruce.

Bruce approached quickly. He struck with the bottom of the shaft, knocking the creature back onto the ground. As it strained to get back up, he stamped on its face, slamming its head back down to the dirt. Finally Bruce swung the hammer head of the weapon down onto the creature's face. The metal head landed firmly between its eyes and smashed through the skull.

Connor struck horizontally with a back fist motion. The force of the heavy implement immediately broke the zombie's neck and it dropped back to the ground. Dylan ran forward with his bardiche. With a wide grip on the haft he smashed the wood into his opponent's face, bursting its nose open and throwing the beast back. With the weapon still in motion he shortened his grip and kicked the zombie's stomach, forcing its head forward. Finally he smashed the heavy bardiche down on the exposed back of the head. The sheer blunt force trauma cracked the skull open, the beast twitching as it collapsed.

Christian ran towards his opponent with all the enthusiasm needed, just none of the skill. He closed the distance too fast and before he could swing the bill the creature had taken hold of the shaft. He pushed and pulled against the hold of the zombie, but it wouldn't release.

"Fuck, fuck, get this fucker off me!" shouted Christian.

The man desperately struggled but to no avail. He punched at the creature with his mail re-enforced gloves, but it had little effect, except to keep it from closing a few inches closer. With the push and pull of the creature he was thrown to the floor. Christian was now flat on his black, desperately holding the zombie at arm's length, unable to move.

Bruce drove his weapon into Christian's opponent as it still endeavoured to bite him. The pointed metal crushed into the beast's cheek. Blood spurted from its neck as it slumped over beside the man. Before it could recover Bruce leapt onto his new opponent, punching it continually until he was satisfied that it presented no further threat. Finally he stood back up, admiring the fresh blood on his steel gauntlets that layered on top of the congealed blood he'd gained earlier from the zombie boy.

It had been a brutal afternoon. Bruce had been happy to have received a purpose in life, but he already wanted to sit down and revel in his success.

"Jump in!" shouted Bruce.

He pulled back the tonneau cover on the bed of his car. It was a Holden UTE, a muscle car with a pickup bed for the uninitiated. The car featured a 5.7 litre V8 which made a satisfying sound to Bruce. He considered himself a true adventurer, but his city credentials let him down. The brand new Holden UTE simply contrasted badly to the country desert. The new ride had big rims and a metallic purple spray job.

Bruce jumped into the driver's seat, glad he always kept his beloved car's keys in his pocket. Dylan threw his bardiche into the trunk, before taking shotgun, the others piled into the back. The growly engine roared to life as Bruce looked out at the horde of bloodthirsty creatures up ahead. He already knew the entrance was blocked, but the only safe way out of here was by car, time to find a new route.

The back tyres spun on the tarmac of the car park, a combination of V8 torque and the weight of his passengers. The car finally roared off in a trail of smoke. Bruce checked out every option available to him, burning around the car park, desperately looking for an alternate exit. As he came to one corner of the car park he pulled on the parking brake and slid the car around.

"Fuck, mate. Easy!" shouted Connor.

Dylan was fossicking through the glove box, desperately trying to find something useful.

"Don't you keep a handgun in here, mate?" asked Dylan.

"No mate, because I ain't a gangster!" said Bruce.

"You're fucking useless, mate," said Dylan.

"And where's your machine gun arsehole?" said Bruce.

"That's fair," said Dylan.

The wheels screeched again in wheel spinning fun. Bruce could finally see a way out, even if the rest of his friends and associates could not. The car gained speed quickly as the powerful motor growled. He was accelerating quickly towards a bush on the rim of the car park.

"What the fuck, mate?" said Dylan.

"No choice, mate. There's no way but the hard way!" said Bruce.

He flicked his stereo on. The excessive sound system blurted to life, blaring Airborne louder than any motorist would consider sensible. The zombies were continually changing course to adapt to Bruce's wild changes of direction. They now all headed in one way, the same that he raced towards.

"Hold on!" shouted Bruce.

The Holden hit a grass ramp and smashed through a

bush at high speed. The weight and speed of the vehicle crashed almost effortlessly through the greenery, causing nothing more than superficial damage to the bodywork. Unfortunately, the embankment the other side was rather steep. Going so fast and the sharp depression caused the vehicle to continue on in the open air.

The wheels left the ground by a good few feet as the car flew through the air to freedom before the heavy chassis crashed back to the dirt. As it came down Lee lost his hold and was thrown from the rear bed. He'd not held on as Bruce had insisted. It was only fortunate that the low profile tyres landed on a soft material. Bruce giggled as he saw the pathetic idiot hit the ground behind them as the car powered on into the distance.

"Well at least we lost the arsehole," said Bruce.

Christian and Connor looked back out of the bed to see the worthless man tumble down. There were no zombies within fifty yards of him, so he had a chance. All the men were content that they'd not left him to die, and equally happy to be rid of the fool.

CHAPTER THREE

Alaska, United States

Dr Garcia was dreaming, at least she thought she was. She was floating in a cloud but had no idea why. Something was moving in the distance, she tried to focus on it. It looked like a shadow that was moving from side to side. She blinked her eyes, trying to work out what the peculiar shape could be. From the cloud the shape took form, it was that of a man. She shook, as though moving her head would clear the cloud. All it did though was seem to make the man even closer. Then it dawned on her, she was still in the corridor and that shape wasn't just a man, it was one of those infected people that had attacked them. As adrenaline pumped around her body she snapped out of her delirious state. With her heart pounding, fear kicked in and she shook herself till she started to move. Her mouth was dry and rough, as though she had the worst hangover in her life. Either that or she was dehydrated from not drinking.

Looking down Dr Garcia saw that there were bodies all around her. One was in fact on top of her legs and midriff. With almost superhuman effort she forced her way out from the mess and into the corridor. She looked back at the shape, the man was still there but appeared entranced by something else. She continued her struggle, lifting herself up onto her knees. She must have been there for a while because both her legs had gone to sleep. She hit her legs, making sure it wasn't anything more serious. Yes, she could feel the impact, she just needed to move them and get the blood circulating again.

She looked around the corridor, trying to ascertain what had happened. The last thing she remembered was the fight in the corridor. It looked different now though, the walls were more damaged than before. All along the one side were bullet hole from small arms fire. A small fire burned near the breach where the booby trap had exploded. The floor was packed full of bodies, some were technicians and others were in Hazmat suits. There were trails of blood leading to the elevator and also to the emergency staircase that she had arrived at. Some feeling was now returning to her limbs. She moved her right leg, noticing that she was still wearing her hazmat suit. She looked over to her left leg, the suit was ripped open though she didn't seem to be hurt. Whatever the biological threat had been it was obviously not affecting her, at least she hoped not.

"How long have I been here?" she muttered to herself, "this place looks like a warzone."

A groan came from the far end of the corridor, it was the infected man. It looked like he'd spotted her. He started moving slowly towards her, dragging what looked like a broken leg behind him. Dr Garcia, remembering now the shooting and fighting in the corridor, tried to move away but her legs were still weak. She looked around for any kind of weapon to defend herself with.

The nearest bodies to her were the Hazmat suited guards. She pulled herself past them, looking for a nightstick, torch or ideally a firearm. There was nothing on them. She pulled herself further away, finally spotting a discarded firearm, one of the Scar rifles. She looked back, the infected man had covered half the distance to her and she could now see his face. His skin tone was pale and deathly whilst his mouth was open and baring teeth. From his gums dripped blood, though there was something frightening about the dark gore. She reached out, grabbing at the rifle. Catching the sling she pulled it towards her. Though she hadn't used a firearm for sometime it was a required part of her training for the company. The shooting on the range brought back the basics and in seconds she'd worked out how to release the magazine and checked it had bullets left. She slipped it back into the weapon and then pulled back on the cocking lever. The first bullet slid in and the firearm was ready. She swung around to aim the gun only to find the man was just a few feet away. She panicked and pulled on the trigger, only to feel resistance from the trigger.

"Shit!" she shouted.

Dr Garcia fiddled around with the rifle, searching for the safety. The man was now close enough to grab her so she kicked and tried to drag herself a bit further away. The rifle clicked as she finally found the lever. Without hesitation she pointed the weapon directly at his torso and fired a single shot. The man staggered back a step and then moved back, reaching out with its arms. Bloody drool dripped from its mouth.

"Back off, keep away from me!" she screamed.

She lowered the gun and fired two more rounds, both into the creature's left side. It dropped, falling onto its chest and face. The creature groaned as it deposited blood and drool onto the floor. Dr Garcia dragged herself back even further, now able to lift herself up onto her knee for more accurate shooting. The man got up, his bones creaking as he dragged himself towards her. Now having had enough of her predicament, she aimed the rifle at his head and fired one more shot. The bullet hit below the eye and created an exit wound the size of a golf ball at the back of the head. Bone and flesh sprayed back into the corridor as the thing finally collapsed to the ground.

The corridor was now silent and Dr Garcia, though shocked managed to stand up. She wanted to know what was going on and where everybody was. Looking back the secondary corridor was the only route likely to be of use to her. The elevator was smashed and the last thing she wanted to do was to get stuck in it when things like that infected man were moving around trying to kill her. She pulled the magazine out of the rifle, finding just a single bullet remaining. Sliding it back into the gun she looked around for any more ammunition or weapons on the bodies.

As she moved she noticed one of the bodies was moving, its hand was reaching out, trying to grab at her. A scream escaped her throat as fear gripped her. She stumbled backwards only to spot movement coming from the damaged room. Lifting the rifle up, she aimed it carefully. A hand appeared, followed quickly by two heads. As the things emerged more hands appeared. There must be a number of them in the room she thought, and she had just the one bullet.

She moved towards the airlock door system that led to the upper stairwell. It was her only chance to avoid them. The door was already open, though it looked suspiciously like it had been forced. Lowering the rifle she moved into the doorway, looking for any problems. Along the wall and floor were streaks of blood, as though somebody had been dragged as they bled. The airlock system was smashed open and clear, leading directly out into the staircase. Moving up the stairs she followed the blood trail, her heart rate racing ahead. As she approached the last few steps she paused, waiting and listening for what might lie ahead. There was no sound, though like the corridor the place looked ramshackle and rundown. Taking a deep breath she moved up the last few steps and turned the corner. The door was shut and locked.

For a moment she panicked, thinking she was trapped between the door and creatures. Reaching out to the door she tried the handle and found to her relief that it was unlocked. Breathing a sigh of relief she moved inside quickly and turned back to shut the door. Coming up the stairs were half a dozen of the infected, perhaps more. Slamming the door she pulled the catch that pulled two sturdy reinforced bars across it. It should be secure, at least for a while.

Safe for the moment she turned around and entered the control room expecting to find Dr Murphy and the rest trying to resolve whatever meltdown scenario was currently going on. The sight that greeted her was shocking. The bodies of technicians, guards and others littered the floor. The power was off or at least most of the lights and equipment weren't running. Nearly all the computer screens were smashed or lying on the floor. Blood seemed to be everywhere and yet not a single living person appeared to be around. There was a foul stench in the air, a gangrenous stink that reminded her of a long rotting carcass.

She crept forwards as slowly and quietly as she could, the sound of her damaged Hazmat suit now seemingly to creak at every movement of her body. Several sets of data and power cables hung from the ceiling and scorch marks nearby signalled the use of stun grenades. A screen was flashing in the corner of the room and it looked like the only working terminal in the building. Scanning the area carefully as she moved, she headed in its direction. Sparks flashed from damaged electronics and the main viewscreen, that she'd been looking at earlier with Dr Murphy, was on the floor in pieces.

"Dr Murphy," she gasped, "where is he?"

Most of the bodies seemed to be general staff and security personnel. Perhaps he'd escaped she thought, or he could be in another part of the building. Her attention returned to the terminal, if she could access the system she might be able to find out what had happened. Moving up to the terminal she was relieved to see it was still active and showed two viable connections. Checking over her shoulder she was about to log in to the system when she spotted the date and time.

"Holy shit!" she exclaimed.

She'd been in the corridor a lot longer than she thought. Almost fifty hours! No wonder she was so parched, she needed food and water, and fast. Shaking her head she logged in using her maximum-security pass and waited. After what seemed like an age it was authenticated and she gained access to what was still running in the centre. With a few clicks she checked on the status of the research centre's facilities. A page of icons and figures popped up, the majority of which were showing red. She ran her hand down the page, examining the data.

"Shit, shit, shit!" she swore.

Only two of the servers were still running and the second one was hitting read errors on its data stores, presumably from damage sustained in the attacks. The security network was down and therefore so was the secure entry point to the main facility building. The perimeter security facilities showed as offline, but that could mean they were either damaged or had been intentionally disabled. The emergency stairwell to the rooftop was blocked or damaged but apparently the main elevator was still online. She put in her secure code and accessed the internal camera feed. More of the video points were offline but there were still six cameras showing as online and transmitting.

Dr Garcia clicked on the first one, it popped up on the screen in a separate window, there was nothing but static. Either the camera was blocked or there was a problem with the connection. The second and third cameras were not much better. She sighed as she clicked on the fourth and fifth, expecting nothing. The windows lit up giving her a view of the foyer and an external feed from the building. She slumped back into her chair at the view. The foyer was in a worse state than the room she was in now. There were several bodies slumped down and at least a dozen blood trails leading outside into the snow. The doors were smashed and there was broken glass and equipment everywhere.

She clicked on the fifth camera, making it full screen to get a better view outside. As usual, there was snow everywhere. The camera was ultra wide angle and showed both part of the outside of the building and also the access road to the security gate. There were vehicle markings where it looked like a number of vehicles had passed in the last day.

Off to the side of the screen was a large vehicle. She double clicked on it to zoom in. The screen blurred for a moment as the camera adjusted and then it focused on the subject. It was a military truck, though it was on its side and from what she could make out there were at least three bodies nearby. The bodies looked like they were wearing military camouflage.

Dr Garcia reduced the size of the screen and examined the sixth and final camera. The view it displayed made her heart race uncontrollably. The camera was in the corridor opposite from the room she was in and led directly to the elevator and emergency stairwell. In the space were scores of people, all with the same undead look as those below. They must have been trying to get out of the building and had been stuck in that area. They didn't seem to be doing anything, just wandering around and touching the walls and lift, presumably trying to work out how to get out. She deduced that only a number of them had managed to get to the foyer using the elevator, probably falling against it or hitting the correct button by mistake. Either way, it meant there were a number of these zombie-like things blocking her route.

She hit a key and brought up a plan of the building. The corridor was definitely now the only route out of the building for her, as the secondary stairwell was blocked by debris and still on fire. Her only other option was to go back down the stairwell to where she'd woken up. That was pointless though as it was a sealed environment with no way out.

A window popped up, it stated it was an emergency call from Dr Murphy. She hit the button, activating a remote video conference. A window appeared showing the doctor and several other people in a vehicle.

"Dr Murphy?" asked a bewildered Dr Garcia.

"Holy shit, Anna, you're alive!" came the response.

"Just about, what happened here? The systems are offline and the place is crawling with crazies."

Dr Murphy nodded into the camera.

"Yeah, the shit has hit the fan. I mean really hit the

fan. I've requested an evac team to get you out. They'll be there in twenty minutes. Are you okay until then?"

She was stunned for a moment, confused at seeing these people after the insanity of the last hours and days.

"I think so. There are lots of those things on the data centre floor. I've locked them out but there are still more in the access corridor," she advised.

"Listen, have you been bitten?" he asked anxiously.

"Bitten? No, I'm fine. Bitten by what, those people?" she asked in a confused voice.

"Yes, those things. Be very careful. Do you know what is going on out here?" he asked.

She turned her head, "No idea."

"Ok, here is the short version. The accident in the data centre has somehow caused a chain reaction. It started with those killed in the blast and from the chemicals. Somehow they aren't dying, or maybe they are and then are being reanimated in some way," he explained.

"What the hell?" she yelled.

"I know, it sounds insane, but look at this," he said.

The view on the screen changed as he moved his handset to show outside the vehicle. She looked carefully, it was the skyline of a city and yet dozens of columns of smoke were climbing up into the sky. Dr Murphy appeared back in view.

"Everything has gone to shit. Those things managed to break out from the centre and infected a few people at the Memorial Airport. From what we can work out the incubation time is about forty-eight hours and the infection is terminal. When you die you become one of those things," he said.

Dr Garcia was stunned and she simply stared at the screen.

"We had to abandon the complex because of the biological hazard. In the last forty-eight hours we think the infection has spread to the United States and to Europe. It's getting out of control. We need you back to help with a response."

"Where are you?" asked Dr Garcia.

I'm heading to one of the research vessels, The Moreau. It has moved offshore to keep away from this shit storm. Wait for the evac team. They'll make sure you join us there."

He turned away, looking at something before returning to the screen.

"I need to go, there are reports the infection has hit London. The team are arriving now, they'll meet you in the foyer, be careful."

She nodded into the screen, "Wish me luck."

The display faded, leaving just the company logo on the terminal screen.

Dr Garcia thought about what was happening. The entire ordeal was insane at best. She was interrupted from her thoughts though by the sound of gunfire coming from the speakers. The change from total silence to what sounded like a battle outside the centre was a shock to her system. She hit the key for the external camera which displayed a Sikorsky UH-60 Black Hawk helicopter emblazoned with the company markings. The aircraft was a four-bladed, twin-engine, medium-lift utility helicopter that was used by both military and civilian operators.

It was sat outside the centre on the landing pad. About a dozen heavily armed men, each wearing high tech body armour and helmets were moving around it, some of them firing at targets outside the compound. The remainder stormed inside the building through the smashed entrance. About a dozen shots fired along with what sounded like heavier weapons.

"Thank God for that, they must be the evac team," she whispered to herself.

She hit the button to bring up the corridor outside her room. It showed the infected moving towards the elevator. They looked agitated but more importantly, they were far enough away from the sealed access door to the stairwell. If she was quick she might be able to use the arrival of the men as a diversion.

The creatures on the lower stairwell must have heard the commotion because the banging on the door started to get louder. A splinter of material tore off to reveal a gap the size of a fist. Blood dripped down it as the creatures continued to smash flesh and bone at the door.

Another hand appeared, the bloodied fingers tearing at the material. At this rate they would be through in just a few minutes.

Making a quick decision she decided it was time to leave. Grabbing her rifle she left the terminal and made straight for the doorway that led to the corridor. Opening it a crack she checked on the creatures. As expected they were all up near the elevator and banging on the smashed glass and control panel. It was only a matter of time before they hit the correct key and moved themselves up to the top floor. Before she could get any further in her escape the door to the lower stairwell smashed open. The creatures having finally ripped their way through it poured inside. The leading creatures fell down, the weight of numbers behind them pushing over them as they swarmed into the control room. Ignoring them, Dr Garcia threw open the door and ran down the corridor. She had no choice now. It was either run or be killed. As she reached the secure doorway to the upper stairwell she was finally spotted by some of the things at the elevator. They turned and wailed at her, drawing her to the attention of the rest.

Dr Garcia put in the emergency override combination and swung the door open just in time to avoid being grabbed by the creatures. She tried to shut the door but it was too late, the number of them pushing at the door made it impossible. Abandoning it she ran up the staircase and towards the foyer. As she came closer to the ground floor above her the sound of boots and gunfire became louder. She opened the door as quickly as she could and moved out into the foyer. It was exactly as it looked on the camera, apart from the corners of the room where the angle of the cameras stopped them from seeing into the shadows. She could see what had kept the guards occupied, as there were dozens of the creatures, some stood and others climbing out from behind smashed terminals. Two of the guards moved towards her, moving in quickly to protect her and not a moment too soon. The door to the stairwell burst open and the horde poured into the room.

The leader of the security team moved close to her, "Dr Garcia?" he asked.

She nodded, too exhausted and shocked to say much more.

"I'm Security Chief Hans, I have orders to evacuate you and any survivors to The Moreau," he explained.

The other members of the team formed a defensive line in front of them as they emptied bullets into the creatures. Though they were able to force them back, the creatures seemed to be able to sustain awful injuries before finally dying.

"Come on!" ordered Hans, holding out his hand to her.

Dr Garcia held on as the group rushed out through the smashed door and into the snow covered parking area. The helicopter was a short distance away but there were also a number of the creatures making their way towards the noise of the machine. The security team kept shooting, their accurate fire clearing a path for the Hans and Dr Garcia. In just a few more seconds they were at the door and Hans helped her into the aircraft. He turned back, adding fire to that of his men. He gave the signal and they began to fall back. A gunner on the helicopter swung his M249 light machine gun towards the building and fired long bursts at the creatures. The rest of the tactical unit retreated, the creatures hot on their heels. With just a few more shots the rest of the men were at the helicopter and jumped in, thankfully with no casualties. With a simple hand signal Hans let the pilot know they were clear and the Black Hawk lifted up into the dark sky.

Dr Garcia slumped back, still unable to believe what she had just gone through. Hans leaned forwards, putting a headset unit on her head. His voice came through clearly.

"Are you ok, Doctor, are you uninjured?" he asked.

Dr Garcia nodded.

Hans turned and pulled out what looked like a tablet computer. He pressed a few keys and handed it over to her. She looked at it intently. It was a summary of all the current news reports and feeds. The first words to catch her attention were those about London. It read that the Prime Minister was injured and that it was being blamed on terrorist action. Sliding the story to one side she checked the next one, it described an attack by a group of rabid men in a large train station in France. It said dozens were hurt and several killed. Each article seemed to be saying the same thing, there were crazed people attacking their neighbours for no apparent reason. As she read further, more stories popped up. It was spreading and spreading fast.

She looked out through the small windows of the helicopter, the landscape was featureless, and this was hardly a state full of monstrous cities. There was just one question on her mind.

"Hans. How did this spread so fast?" she asked.

"No idea, Doctor. From the reports I've seen, it seems that the common link is the airport here in Barrow. The people with the infection can apparently carry the condition for two days before you can see any difference," he said.

The helicopter climbed up higher until above the clouds and continued its progress towards the ship. Dr Garcia turned back to the tablet, reading the most recent story.

It simply read, 'Zombie Apocalypse hits Manhattan'. Along the scrolling ticker at the bottom of the page was the message that the governor had declared a state of emergency.

"Zombies?" cried Dr Garcia as she almost choked on her own words.

CHAPTER FOUR

Berkshire, England

The sun beat down upon the large glass windows and flies buzzed around in the annoying manner that they always do. It was another depressing Monday. Dave lay back in his leather chair which was frayed at the edges and the cushion flattened from years of use. He'd worked in this concrete tower for six years, bored to death. The sound of colleagues toiling away on utterly pointless, brain numbing work. For just a few moments his mind wandered from the office hell to a better place, just dreaming of the cool beer he lusted after.

"Dave!" shouted Jones.

The boss's voice rang out from across the room. The cheap suit buying, BMW driving, golf loving, pink shirt wearing, lower management asshole was stood at the water cooler. He'd spotted Dave's slackened posture and been all too fond to call him up on the fact.

"Isn't it about time you got some work done?" said Jones.

The idiot had deliberately said it from across the room, loud enough for everyone to witness, they all hated him as much as Dave did, but that didn't stop him making examples of colleagues on a regular basis, and getting a kick out of it. Dave said nothing, but simply sat more upright at his desk and pretended to give a damn. His workstation really was rubbish, an old grey dreary desk with horribly outdated equipment. The keyboard was stained yellow from age. The monitor was the same 16" CRT that he'd used when starting the position, this really was a dead end job.

"Did you not get the memo?" said Jones in a smarmy tone.

"Memo?"

Dave knew about the memo, but he would never give Jones the satisfaction of knowing it. That bastard would be an anal git about every potential issue he could, just to make full use of the little power he held.

"Employees are not to tilt back on their chairs. It's a health and safety hazard. Any and all injuries or damage of equipment as a result of doing so will be at the employee's expense and liability," said Jones.

Dave could do or say nothing without bringing down

the wrath of the utter bastard, so he simply nodded and carried on with his work. Jones stood upright triumphantly and looked out across the miserly amount of office space he controlled, as smug as ever.

"Where's Chris?" said Jones.

He was his usual obnoxious self. Chris's seat was empty, his computer not even turned on. The man had clearly never arrived at work. Chris was a decent chap, not all that interesting, but friendly. He liked nothing more than to simply lay about the house, have the odd BBQ and watch the footie. But Dave knew for a fact that he'd been on a weekend away to Benidorm with his girlfriend, so was probably wasted. Dave felt sorry for Chris already, fully understanding the painfully annoying rant he would receive.

"Did Chris sign in this morning?" asked Jones.

The office only had fifteen computers in it and just as many workers. It was astonishing it had taken Jones an hour to notice someone was missing. He was probably busy tough talking his nancy boy henchmen, the pathetic creatures who would lick his boots for a good word. The room looked around at Jones, a few muttered, but nobody committed to a real answer. In all honesty, Dave wasn't even sure if he had seen Chris today, as his mind had just switched off to the boredom of the nine to five. Jones picked up a nearby phone, not caring to make the call private, it was for all to hear.

"Chris? You're an hour late for work, what the hell do you think you're doing?"

You would think the world was in danger from the lack of Chris's presence, but no, he was just late for more endlessly pointless and boring work.

"I don't care how rough you feel, you didn't call in sick, stop giving me excuses and take some responsibility, get here now!"

Jones slammed the phone down and walked out of the room, clearly going to ensure Chris had the hour docked from his salary, and a mark against his record. Another two hours went by, sweat dripped from Dave's face on to his poorly ironed white shirt. He mindlessly entered data, not even sure anymore if the work actually achieved anything, or if he was simply employed for the sake of it. Perhaps its purpose was to fulfil some requirement of the business, or maybe to help avoid the upper management assholes some tax that they should be paying. The reason for his work simply didn't matter anymore, he got paid, that was all that was important, and at least he had a job.

Desperate for the toilet, having drunk too much coffee to try and survive the morning, Dave walked off to the men's room. Standing at the urinal he sighed in relief, it was the best feeling all day. Walking over to the wash basins he looked out the window down onto the street below. An ambulance and police car were parked up on the pavement, lights still flashing. Two coppers nearby were beating a man on the floor with their truncheons.

"Bastards, if only I could get my hands on you," said Dave.

He left the toilets and headed back to his desk. Despite still being in full stride, he was simply on autopilot. Dave was day dreaming, just thinking of Stallone in Rambo II shooting up the office with his M60. It was a pleasant thought, and one he only wished he could replicate. Getting back to his desk, the bored IT worker slumped back into his chair, back to the boring reality of work.

Chris finally walked into the office, he was pale and even sweatier than the rest, he looked terrible, but no one spoke a word to him. Nobody wanted to risk having a verbal beating from Jones. Finally, it was lunch time. Not a second had gone past twelve before the entire room stood and headed for the canteen.

"Chris, you haven't put an ounce of work into this day, you can use your lunch break to make up at least some of the time you've lost," said Jones.

What a swine, everyone thought it, no one said it. The room cleared as Chris sat back down, he really was ill enough that he should be at home, but Jones wouldn't let that fact reduce his bad attitude. To be fair, his sickness was probably self-inflicted. You cannot expect to rush off for a drunken weekend and then return on a Monday morning in a workable state. None of this changed the fact that Jones was a complete nob.

In the canteen Dave sat down with the two colleagues that he at least had some interest in talking to, Barry and James. The three sat around a table, unpacking the contents of the plastic lunch boxes all had brought, as they always did. Half an hour went by of chatting about the usual topics, cars and women. The lunch breaks were the only bearable part of the job, when friends could relax and talk as they wanted. However, they were always too aware that Jones would listen in on a regular basis, desperately trying to dig new dirt on his slaves for later use.

CHAPTER FIVE

Bristol, England

It had been a long morning when Gary and Matt pulled up at McDonalds to get their lunch. The two police officers had worked together for two years now, quickly becoming close friends, both men were in their thirties. Gary had joined the force with images of high speed chases and action. He loved his action movies and his treasured Ducati superbike. The reality of the job was that he'd never handled a gun and was behind the wheel of a diesel Vauxhall Astra. McDonalds was a completely unglamorous way to spend their break, but it was a routine that they'd fallen into.

The two men got out of their car and strolled over to the front door of the fast food chain. They both wore high visibility stab vests over white shirts. It was too hot for jumpers.

"I've been thinking about this all morning," said Matt.

"Know what you mean, mate," said Gary.

Getting through the glass doors they were confronted with a large queue, they could already feel the gazing stares upon them. Children looked at them out of interest, adults out of disgust, they didn't care.

"Fuck me, I'm starving," said Matt.

"Easy on the language mate, there are kids about," said Gary.

"Nothing they haven't heard before, I'm sure," said Matt.

Gary said no more, he knew it was useless arguing with his friend. Matt often got the two of them into trouble as he would rush headlong into every situation and show few common courtesies.

"Get up to much on the weekend?" asked Matt.

"Went for a ride, took my son to the zoo, watched some TV, that's about it, you?" asked Gary.

"Not a lot, spent most of it watching Dave," said Matt.

"What a waste," said Gary.

"What?" asked Matt.

"Well all you do is whine all week that you're bored and then you get to the weekend and do nothing," said Gary.

"Ah, fuck it," said Matt.

They'd been waiting for just two minutes, but it felt much longer. They were almost at the front of the queue when the radio on Gary's chest rung out, the unpleasant sound of their lunch break about to be spoiled.

"Fuck me," said Matt.

"Hang on, mate," said Gary.

"We have a riot in progress at the University of the West of England, Frenchay Campus, all officers report immediately to their stations for briefing," the despatch officer said.

"Hell yeah, we may get to beat some student skulls in, that's worth missing lunch for!" said Matt.

The people in the queue around the officers looked at Matt in outrage. They couldn't say anything against the authorities without causing themselves difficulty. Gary felt ashamed to be in his friend's presence at this time, but he knew there was nothing he could do or say to either calm the situation or change Matt. In all honesty, despite Gary not liking Matt's verbal response, the opportunity of some action was an appealing one. The two men rushed out of the establishment to their car.

Gary leapt into the driving seat and put his foot to the floor. The small diesel engine was nothing special, but the officers had learned to ring every last drop of power from it. The front wheels squealed as they screamed out of the car park. Matt hit the lights and siren whilst Gary passed through every red light, fully enjoying doing so. Within minutes the men were at their station, eagerly running through the front doors. The station was a small one with just eight field officers on duty. They were greeted by their sergeant, Richards.

"Gary, Matt, get your gear on sharpish, you have five minutes," said Richards.

The two men rushed to their lockers. Their riot gear was thrown in there untidily, they'd never had much use for it. Neither of them had worn riot kit since training and they quickly put it all on. It was the fastest the two men had done anything in their job, finally finding motivation when a few skulls needed beating. After just a few minutes the two men were fully kitted and ready to move. They had full riot protection on, helmets in hand. They followed the sergeant and other men to one of the vans and jumped in. The van raced off with the blue lights flashing.

"So what's the deal Sarge?" asked Matt.

"All we know is that a riot has broken out at the university campus. The first officers on the scene came under attack and have not been in contact. We don't know the reason for the riot or the current status."

"So we're going in blind?" asked Gary.

"Exactly, a number of other forces will be joining us there. Firearms units have been called in, but we don't have an ETA on them as yet," said Richards.

"So do we have any idea on the number of rioters?" asked Gary.

"No. Our job is to contain the scenario and assist any officers still on the scene," said Richards.

"Are we authorised to strike first?" asked Gary.

"No, we wall off the area and take it from there," said Richards.

"Fucking great, so our guys get the shit kicked out of them, but we can't return the favour?" asked Matt.

"Stop that shit, Matt, we have a job to do, we're professionals. I expect all of you to be on top form and to obey the law and my command!" shouted Richards.

The next five minutes of the journey to the university were a mix of emotions. The adrenaline was fuelling all of the men, but the lack of information also worried them. In this age of communication and technology they were not used to going into a major disturbance and with such little info.

Looking out of the window of the van, they were just a few hundred yards from the scene now. A small number of people were running or staggering away with torn, blood stained clothes. Clearly this was not a peaceful protest.

Finally the van came to a halt at the small roundabout which led to the campus entrance and the eight men got out of the vehicle. Each was equipped from head to toe in their standard riot control equipment. They also carried translucent round shields and batons. Richards had the loudhailer in hand and looked out at the scene of horror.

A crowd of people were walking slowly towards them, many covered in blood. They weren't carrying banners or shouting abuse, it was an eerie scene. None of the men other than the sergeant had experience of a riot, but all knew too well that this was no ordinary scene.

"This is the police, stop where you are!" shouted Richards down the loudhailer.

There was no answer from the crowd who simply shambled on towards them, now two hundred yards away. Everything about this scene unsettled the men, but they stood their ground. A second police van raced on to the scene, seven men joining the group.

"What the fuck is going on?" asked Matt.

"I don't know, Gary, take the loudhailer, see what you can do," said Richards.

The sergeant ran to the second vehicle to make contact with the new officers.

"Chaps, I cannot tell you anything more about this than you already know and can see, please get in front of our van and bolster my men, I'm going to see if I can get some contact with despatch. I don't know what's going on here but it's going to get bad," said Richards.

The new coppers simply nodded and ran to join the other officers. They likely would have had a lot more questions had they seen the crowd bearing down on the first group. Richards jumped into the van they'd come in.

"Despatch, we have a situation here, please advise," said Richards.

"Rioting has spread across the city, the station is under

attack, we'll not hold out for long," said the despatch officer.

"Tina, is that you? What the fuck is going on?" shouted Richards.

"I honestly don't know, people have gone crazy, they've broken through the doors! Good luck, Sir," said the despatch officer.

"Tina? Tina!" shouted Richards.

There was no response. He jumped out of the vehicle and walked in front of his men. Gary was still shouting at the crowd in an attempt to make them stop.

"Our station is under attack by rioters like this. Only, I am not convinced these are rioters. This problem has spread across the city like wildfire. We're now on our own. We can either stay and fight or try and help the staff left at our station."

"Let's get back to base, work out what the fuck is going on," said Gary.

Richards looked at the sergeant of the other group.

"I suggest you attend to your own people," said Richards.

"Agreed, good luck," said the sergeant.

The two groups piled into their vehicles and were again on the move, just thirty yards away from the crowd that was bearing down on them. The tyres screeched as both vans rushed off.

"What the fuck is going on?" asked Matt.

"No idea, it's like the city has gone mad, civilians are attacking and killing people. We no longer have any control," said Richards.

"So, what, the country has suddenly gone to war with itself?" asked Gary.

"It would seem so. Communication lines have broken down, I'd heard of unusual isolated reports of attacks leading up to this afternoon, it's likely related," said Richards.

"What do we do?" said Gary.

"Let's get back to the station and see what we can do to help," said Richards.

"And what about the fuckers who want to hurt us?" said Matt.

"Don't hit first, but respond if attacked," said Richards.

Gary looked out of the window. Despite the van being pushed to beyond the speed limits, cars were passing them. Clearly nobody cared for the law anymore. They reached a roundabout, stopping to check if they could drive on. A saloon on the roundabout veered out of control whilst taking the bends too fast and clipped a white van, sending it tumbling into the police vehicle. The officers' van was thrown onto its side. It was only fortunate that they had their helmets still on that saved Garry and Matt serious injury. Gary came to his senses a few minutes later. He looked around. Four of the eight officers had been killed outright by the van which had collided with the side of their vehicle at high speed. He could feel aches and pains running through his body. The sliding door to the van was open, facing up to the sky. Gary could see that Richards was stood on top of the vehicle getting access to the driver's compartment. He looked around and could see Matt next to him, eyes shut but he wasn't moving. He tapped his friend's helmet.

"Matt! Matt!" shouted Gary.

His friend awoke, still dazed.

"What happened?" asked Matt.

"We were hit by a van, we have to move!" said Gary.

He got up and helped Matt to his feet. They grabbed a few shields and batons and threw them out the open hatch onto the road before heaving themselves out. Richards was trying to pull the body of the driver, Jacob, out of his seat.

"What are you doing?" asked Gary.

"Jacob is dead, but Rob is stuck down there in the passenger seat, give me a hand," said Richards.

It was a dreadful thing to have to do. All of them were friends, and they had been talking to Jacob just minutes before. Now they had to haul his dead body out of a wrecked vehicle, to be tossed aside. Gary took hold of Jacob's body armour with Richards and yanked his body out of the cab, tumbling it off the vehicle onto the road. They reached in and pulled Rob up out of the vehicle. His leg was cut and bleeding.

"Can you walk?" asked Richards.

"Not sure, I'll do what I can," said Rob.

The men clambered from the smashed vehicle onto the road. Rob winced in agony as he landed on his injured leg. They took up the batons and shields from the ground.

"Can you walk or not?" asked Richards.

"I don't think so, Sarge," said Rob.

"Matt, Gary, give him some help," said Richards.

Richards looked around the area. Cars still whizzed in and around the wreckage of the vehicles, none stopped to give assistance. In all directions what they knew as rioters were shambling about. Most of these people were covered in blood and they seemed to amble aimlessly around.

"We can be at the station in five to ten minutes if we get a shift on," said Richards.

The group set off towards their destination. It was hot and tiring to be constantly on the move in full riot gear, but with people being attacked all around they were glad of the protection. Whilst Gary and Matt helped Rob keep up, Richards took point.

Richards was a capable man and his anger at what had happened to his officers was about to be unleashed on anyone who dared get in their way. They took a bend to see three people in their path.

"Step aside!" shouted Richards

The people didn't respond. Their skin was pale and oddly wrinkled, their clothes torn. Blood was all over their clothing and they staggered towards the group. They appeared to no longer be human, but brain dead, yet they moved with purpose.

"Stand aside or we will use force!" said Richards.

The people gave out groans and didn't stop. Richards was not ever a man of violence, but these people were responsible for the deaths of his friends and fellow officers. He went forward with his shield and baton at the ready. He slammed the baton into the stomach of the first, causing it to keel over. Before it could recover he hit the back of the shoulder blades, sending the man tumbling to the ground.

He struck the legs of the next person, a woman. The baton struck her knee cap sending her tumbling to the pavement. Finally he slammed his shield into the third one and shoved him up against the building next to them.

"Why are you doing this? What is the purpose?" asked Richard.

The man didn't reply, but stared into Richards's eyes. His jaw opened and he fought against his hold, but couldn't break free of the position he was wedged into. The two people on the floor were already getting up, as if they hadn't even noticed the injuries or pain they'd received.

"Hold on to him," said Matt.

Gary held Rob up as Matt stepped in to help Richards. The woman whose knee was knackered was kneeling, unable to get back up because of the joint injury. Matt kicked her in the face with his steel toe capped boot, her nose exploded in blood as she was thrown onto her back. He twisted around and smashed his baton horizontally into the other's face, breaking his jaw.

"Have that you bastards!" shouted Matt.

"What are these people?" asked Richards.

"Look like zombies to me, Sarge," said Matt.

"Don't be ridiculous, this isn't a movie. We're in a shit storm and you're living in TV land again," said Richards.

"He's right, I don't know how or why, but look at the facts," said Gary.

"Sounds like shite to me, but fuck it, I've had enough," said Richards.

He swung his baton down onto the man's head and it connected with force, making his body go limp against the shield. He pulled it back and the body slumped to the ground. The two other attackers were already trying to get back up, ignoring their injuries.

"Fuck this, let's move on, leave those two," said Richards.

"What?" said Matt.

"We've done enough damage already, I want some more answers before we start killing and maiming more civilians," said Richards.

"Well fuck that, these are animals," said Matt.

"You don't know that, get going, that's an order," said Richards.

The four men moved on, despite the two people doing

their utmost to get back on their feet to take hold of them. Fortunately, for whatever reason, they were too slow to keep up with the group. About three hundred yards on they could see a man on the ground, he was still moving slightly, clearly injured. They approached him with caution.

Richards knelt down beside the man. He'd clearly been bitten on the side of the neck, a deep wound. Blood was pouring from it. He was desperately trying to apply pressure to stop the bleeding but he was getting weaker. Seeing the policeman kneel beside him he tried to ask for help, but couldn't get a word out.

Richards knew it was too late for the man, but he put pressure on his throat, simply so the man could die knowing he wasn't alone. A few seconds later the light from the man's eyes faded and he stopped moving completely, his arms went limp. Richards looked up at his friends, sorrowful. It was truly a dark day.

"What the hell is going on here?" asked Richards.

"It's the end of the world," said Rob.

"Quit that religious crap, mate, nobody buys it," said Matt.

"But it's an apocalypse," said Rob.

The dead man suddenly awoke and grabbed Richards's hand and bit hard into the glove. The Kevlar re-enforced gloves had substantial slice protection and blunt trauma to the back of the hand, but the palms were thin, affording a good grip. The man's lower jaw pierced the glove and drove into his palm. The sergeant gave out a cry of pain.

"You fucker!" shouted Richards.

He picked up his baton and slammed it into the man's forehead, knocking him back to the ground. He hit him again and again until the man's face was flattened and a bloodied pulp. He finally stopped the onslaught and stood up, cradling his wounded left hand.

"What the hell just happened?" asked Richards.

"He was a zombie," said Matt.

"What do you mean was a zombie?" asked Gary.

"That man died and came back to life as a biting fucker," said Matt.

"What does all this mean?" asked Richards.

"All those bitten by zombies become them," said Matt.

"Bullshit, according to who?" asked Richards.

"Look I didn't make up the rules, that's what happens in the movies," said Matt.

"It would explain how this riot turned into a fully fledged disaster so quickly," said Gary.

"So am I just going to die and then come back to life?" asked Richards.

"We don't know that yet," said Rob.

"Fuck this, let's go," said Richards.

Matt and Gary shot a look at each other. Richards was the smartest and toughest man they'd known, but he may have just succumbed to the disease that would make him a flesh eating monster, it was a troubling thought. They finally reached the station where they were based. The main door was smashed, the windows too. A thing, like the last ones, stood outside the building.

"What do we do?" asked Matt.

"About the zombie?" asked Richards.

"Kill the bitch," said Gary.

"Well go on then, it's your turn to get your hands dirty," said Richards.

The zombie, who appeared to be a woman in her late forties, turned when hearing the men. She snarled at the group before shambling towards them and raised her arms in anticipation.

"Hold on to Rob," said Gary.

Matt took Rob's weight onto his shoulder whilst Gary approached the zombie. He swung the shield into her arms, crushing them, whilst exposing her temple as she was forcibly turned. He smashed the truncheon down onto the side of her head with all the force he had. The precise blow downed his foe immediately, blood dripping from the gaping wound.

"Let's go," said Gary.

They walked through the demolished station entrance to try and find any survivors. The station was a wreck, paper and stationery strewn everywhere. Patches of blood were scattered across the floor and along the walls. There had clearly been quite a fight there. Gary could hear some noise in one of the offices around the corner.

He moved quickly towards the sound. As he got to the door he bumped into Tina, knocking both of them to the ground.

"Sorry, Tina," he said.

He stumbled to his feet and looked up at his colleague who was dragging herself upwards at a nearby desk. As he moved to help her she shot a look at him. Blood oozed from her mouth and throat, her eyes were bloodshot, crazy.

"Tina, are you still in there?" asked Gary.

There was no response. She finally straightened up and stared at him. Her arm lifted as if to reach for him, but she was a few feet away.

"Tina, please answer me!" shouted Gary.

The other men arrived in the room to see the bloody mess that Tina was in.

"Fuck, she's gone, mate," said Matt.

Tina began stumbling towards the men, a few steps and she'd be on them.

"Gary, sort her out!" shouted Richards.

Gary grabbed his truncheon from the floor.

"Sorry Tina, I never wanted this," said Gary.

He hit her hard across the head sending her tumbling to her knees and exposing the back of her head. He finally smashed down the weapon on her and she fell lifeless to the floor.

They all sat down on the desk tops, staring at each other

with forlorn expressions.

"What's the plan, Sarge?" asked Matt.

"First, it's about time you got used to someone else being in charge," said Richards.

The men all sat solemnly for a minute before Rob finally broke the silence.

"You don't know that you'll become one of them," said Rob.

"Yes we do! We've seen the evidence with our very eyes. Every minute I stay around you is taking us closer to disaster. Either you leave me behind or kill me, those are the options," said Richards.

"No, fuck that! I won't believe it! Gary, you don't believe that do you?" said Matt.

Gary pulled his riot helmet off and wiped his sweaty brow with the sleeve of his boiler suit. He didn't want to give any answer to this, but it was quickly becoming clear that he was going to have to take command of the situation.

"Richards is right, none of us wants to accept it, but a bite from those fuckers is the end for any of us," said Gary.

"No way, man. He's still living and breathing," said Rob.

Richards grabbed Rob by the chest plate of his body armour in anger. The man was shocked and surprised.

"Listen to me, I'm finished, you must move on, survive,

that's an order!" shouted Richards.

Rob didn't respond. None of them had ever questioned their orders, and despite them knowing in the back of their minds that he was right, none wanted to accept the fact.

"So what's your plan?" Richards asked.

"My wife and son, I must reach them," said Gary.

"What about you two?"

"My family live in Northumberland, not much I can do right now," said Rob.

"I'm single, and don't have a family," said Matt.

He was a cynical bastard, but he happened to be correct. Matt's parents were killed in a car crash a few years earlier, and he never was one to settle down.

"Then go with Gary, help him save his family, and then get to safety," said Richards.

"Where is safe?" asked Matt.

"I honestly don't know. Either head for the country where there are fewer people and maybe less problems, or hold up somewhere secure where you have lots of supplies. Hopefully, if you can survive long enough, the military will get things under control. Be under no illusions, this is potentially the start of an apocalypse, you must do everything you can to survive," said Richards.

"What will you do?" asked Gary.

"I suppose I'll put my feet up, have a coffee and watch the world go by," said Richards.

His cool resolve had stayed true to the end. It was a

hard decision for the sergeant to make, to choose to be left behind. Every part of him wanted to carry on with his friends, but he knew better. Despite this deep sadness, the hardened copper would never let his friends see weakness.

"It's time we left, grab the keys to one of the cars," said Gary.

Matt took the keys from reception for one of the squad cars out on the road. They were fortunate for this respite, but it was time to get on with their task, to Gary's family. Matt helped Rob back to his feet and they began to move out of the building.

"Good luck, all of you," said Richards.

"And to you, Sarge, thank you," said Gary.

Getting to the door of the station they could see a group of zombies shambling forwards, between them and the car.

"Hey Sarge, how about one last fight?" asked Matt.

"Gladly," said Richards.

The four men drew their truncheons and held up their shields. Rob could stand and fight, he only had a problem covering distance. Richards went forward first, no longer having any fear of death or injury, only a bitter hatred of the enemy. He swung his baton horizontally into the first creature's face, sending it spinning on its feet. Before the beast could tumble to the ground he smashed the baton down on its skull. The neck jolted and the zombie crumpled to the ground.

Gary drove forwards, he smashed the first beast in the face with the rim of his shield. The round riot shields they carried were light, less than a kilo each, but they were enough to control an opponent. With his first target sent flying backwards onto the tarmac, Gary spun around and smashed his truncheon onto the back of another creature's head. As the zombie slumped over, he kicked it in the face with his steel toe capped boots. Blood spurted from its crumpled face as it flew onto its back. Before it could recover, Gary swung his baton down onto its skull, trapping it between the weapon and ground. The strong downward blow immediately fractured the skull.

Matt charged at his target, screaming. He barged into the zombie with his shield, driving it to the boot of the car they were intending to take. The strong charge forced the creature's spine onto the edge of the car, with Matt's bodyweight forcing its torso to arch over the vehicle, breaking its back. The spine cracked with an unpleasant sound, but Matt didn't hesitate. He used his truncheon with a hammerfist blow twice on its head. The strong strikes bloodied its face and dented the boot of the car. Finally he swung the baton around and brought it down full force onto the beast's skull. The zombie slumped down onto Matt, but he just stepped back in disgust, allowing it to topple to the street.

Rob hobbled forward, unable to keep up with the speed his friends had attacked with. He smacked the first target he could reach with his truncheon, but he was tackled from his shield side. With his injured leg Rob couldn't stay standing and tumbled to the ground. He hit at the creature that had knocked him down. As he tried to fight his new target, it reached his legs and bit into his thigh in a gap between his armour. The man screamed out in agony. Lifting his upper body he hit down on the base of the skull of his new attacker until blood poured out across the ground.

Gary looked down the street from where they'd come from, an ever growing horde was approaching.

"Get to the car and get out of here!" shouted Richards.

The sergeant helped Rob to his feet whilst Matt and Gary kept fighting wildly.

"Get going now!" shouted Richards.

Gary looked around, he was finally beginning to understand the necessity of survival at any cost. There was no glory in a last stand when no man on earth would be alive to remember it.

"Matt, come on!" shouted Gary.

Gary clicked the remote control to open the car and charged at a creature blocking his path, he lowered his head and rammed its skull head first with his riot helmet. The zombie flew several feet into the side of the car. Without stopping Gary rushed at it with his knee, smashing the creature with the robust plastic limb protection he wore. The zombie's head twisted sharply as the blow landed and it slumped to the ground. He opened the door and threw his shield and baton onto the back seat.

Matt leapt onto the car bonnet and slid across it. There was one final creature in his way. He punched it in the face and then beat his baton into its stomach. The zombie dropped down. Matt swung the door open and kicked the beast's head into the doorway before smashing the door shut on its head. He slammed the door continuously until blood seeped down the car sill.

"Get the fuck in the car you idiot!" shouted Gary.

Matt threw his stuff in and jumped into the car. The two men looked out at Richards and Rob. The injured men were fighting more than a dozen zombies, with more incoming.

"Give 'em hell!" shouted Gary.

He started the car and immediately slipped the clutch, sending the front wheels into a spin. The car roared off down the road. It would be the last time they saw their friends, at least as they knew them.

CHAPTER SIX

Berkshire, England

They had spent the morning dying of heat and boredom. The three men went out of the canteen and down the corridor towards their office. Jones was already ahead of them, his office being closer than theirs to the canteen. The sleazy boss was probably busy knocking golf balls around his office, never having anything better to do than insult those on a smaller salary.

"Stop that right now! You're a disgrace!" Jones shouted.

Without stopping, all three men ran into the room. Sarah, one of the office girls was lying on top of Chris, her body wriggling. The three colleagues stood not wanting to get involved, but still watching the situation unfold, it would be funny if nothing else. Jones stormed towards the pair, furious. He put his hands onto Sarah's shoulders and pulled her off Chris.

"What the fuck?" said Jones.

Sarah slumped lifeless down to the floor and the others could now see some of what had shocked Jones. Blood poured from her neck, flesh ripped from the throat, her white blouse dripping in her own blood. The same blood trickled from Chris's mouth and he now had a crazy expression on his face. Jones struck out his hand and pointed in anger at him, shouting at the man, his hand and finger shaking as he couldn't control himself.

Chris reached out and took hold of Jones's arm and bit into his index finger before ripping it from the hand. Blood was spurting from the wound as Jones screamed out in agony, clenching his bloody hand with his other. Dave and his friends still stood where they had, unable to move, in total shock. Chris stumbled to his feet.

"What the hell do you think you're doing?" Jones screamed.

The blood soaked employee said nothing, but began staggering towards the panicked boss. Jones turned around to face Dave and his friends, utter shock on his face.

"Do something!" shouted Jones.

Before Dave could even think of a response to the situation Chris pulled Jones back and bit deep into his neck, the man screaming out once again, louder this time. Blood spurted from his neck as Chris drove his teeth in deep. Dave looked around, his two friends had already left the room. Suddenly feeling very vulnerable, he leapt out the doorway and shut it behind him. He rested back against the wall, his two friends there beside him.

"What the hell was that all about?" asked Barry.

"No fucking idea, mate," said James.

"Have you not seen Dawn of the Dead, you idiots?" asked Dave.

"Fuck off! That's just plain silly," said Barry.

"Oh really, so you see people bite each other to death regularly?" Dave said.

The door reverberated as a loud smashing sound rang out from inside the office. The three men jumped at the sudden sound.

"What do we do?" asked James.

"Why are you asking me?" Dave responded.

"Well you watch those kinds of movies," said James.

"But most of the characters in those movies die," said Dave.

"Then do the opposite!"

The beating on the door got louder, as if several people were now attacking it.

"To Jones's office!" shouted Dave.

It was the best thing Dave could think to do. Never investigate in these circumstances, those who do always die in the movies. At least Jones's office would be empty, and he wouldn't need it anytime soon. As the three men ran down the corridor the door behind them burst open, none looked back to observe the scenario. They reached the office and slammed the door quickly behind them.

"Help me move this desk over!" said Dave.

The men slid the table across the entrance, blocking the door.

"What the fuck, mate?" said Barry.

"Turn that radio on!" said Dave.

Screams echoed around the floor of the building, the men each looking at one another in fear and astonishment.

"Hit the radio!" shouted Dave.

"Why?" asked Barry.

"Because I want to know what the hell is going on in the world!" said Dave.

Barry turned the radio on, and the worst kind of modern dance music resonated from the device.

"Radio one, what a faggot," said James.

Quickly twisting the tuning wheel Barry was flicking through stations.

"Barry, seriously, we aren't trying to listen to music, I want to hear the news!"

"I know, I know," said Barry.

He kept flicking the channels of the DAB radio.

"Barry!"

The station flicked on to Planet Rock, with the familiar sound of Saxon airing. Barry looked back with a grin. Dave shook his head at the complete lack of understanding of priorities from his friend. Finally, the track came to a close and it was time for the one o'clock news. The men all stood silently and intently as the screams of panic and pain ran through the seven floors of the building. They were at least partly comforted by the sturdy table which constituted their barricade.

"We're getting reports that following an attack on Parliament just minutes ago there are more than fifty dead and wounded, including injuries to the Prime Minister. No reports have yet given any information about the motive for the attack, though similar violence seen in Canada and France this morning has already led to speculation of terrorist activity," said the news anchor.

"That was no terrorist attack!" said James.

"No, but they clearly don't know that yet," said Dave.

"So what happens now?" asked Barry.

"Well usually people draw guns and start shooting," said Dave.

"This is England, mate. What do we do?" asked James.

An almighty crash resounded from beyond the windows, and sirens could be heard in the distance. They moved to the window to look out across the street. A car was upside down, half resting on another parked at the side of the road. Screams rang out across the street, whilst people ran in all directions.

"What can we do?" asked Barry.

"Well we can't stay here," said Dave.

"Why not?" asked James.

"Look outside, the world has gone to shit, and it's only going to get worse," said Dave

"Right, so what's the plan?" asked Barry.

"Get to my car and get out of here."

"Alright, but how do we get past those things?" asked Barry.

"You mean zombies?"

"Uh, yeh!" said Barry.

"We ask them nicely to move aside. Think you idiot. We kick the shit out of them!"

The two men looked bewildered, but not Dave. He was in his element, bored of the endless toil of his pointless work. He could finally get out some aggression. It was game time.

"Right, so how do we fight them?" asked Barry.

"Find something big and heavy and hit them across the head with it until they stop moving," said Dave.

The men looked around for anything that could serve as a weapon. Barry took hold of a wide branched plant that was more like a small tree, putting it over his shoulder. James took out the golfing umbrella from the coat rack whilst Dave grasped Jones's prized club, a putter he kept about for office games. What a sad bastard.

"Right, you both ready?"

The two men shrugged their shoulders and nodded in some sense of agreement. All of them only wished they lived in a country where men carried guns. Dave took hold of the desk and drew it back. Edging closer to the door, he opened it cautiously and peered out through the gap to the corridor. There was a blood trail running from their office, out past Jones's and around the corner, but no sign of anyone. The three men edged into the corridor.

"Go for the lift," Barry whispered.

"No you idiot, think about that for a minute, we'll take the stairs," said Dave.

James started walking off towards their office, far quicker than they had cautiously left the previous room. Dave stood upright and stared at him in astonishment.

"Where are you going?" Dave insisted.

"To get my coat," he replied.

"Don't be an idiot, it's hot out there anyway," Dave replied.

It was too late. James was already through the door, having followed the trail of blood, something only a fool would do.

"Bloody hell, come on then," Dave said.

Barry and Dave carefully continued on and into the office, the door hanging from the bottom hinge. Getting back into the workplace they had unfortunately become so intimately acquainted with over the last few years, they found nothing of note, except blood. The two watched on as James took his coat from his chair and threw it on, he turned around with a grin on his face, but it quickly turned to a grimace of fear.

"Fuck!" James shouted.

The two men looked around to see the ever cringe worthy sight of the cheap suited Jones, now dripping in fresh blood down his perfectly ironed shirt. Congealed blood was caked around his neck injury, which had all but appeared to have stopped bleeding. The creepy management git didn't say a word, just groaned and began walking towards the men. His right hand was outstretched forward, showing the grizzly stump where the finger had so recently been removed. The two men backed up until finally they bumped into James.

"What now?" asked James.

"Hit the bastard!" yelled Dave.

James went first, using the umbrella like a club, but it just bent and broke over the skull. Barry swung the plant with all his power, using the root and pot end as a weight to bear down on the boss's head. The pot shattered, knocking him down to one knee. Earth poured out across Jones's head, sticking to the blood across his face.

"Fuck this!" shouted Dave.

He threw down the golf club and ran over to his work station. Taking hold of his crappy old CRT monitor and without attempting to unplug anything, he wrenched it up and off the table. Lifting the monitor above his head, Dave ran and smashed the bulky thing onto his boss's head. The monitor completely enveloped it, the rim of it resting on his shoulders. His body twitched before finally collapsing to the floor. Dave looked back at his friend while still standing over the body of his victim.

"That was fucking cool, mate," shouted Barry.

"I'm starting to like this day," replied Dave.

"Time to go," said Barry.

"To the Batmobile!" shouted James.

The three men were walking out of the room and into the corridor, but immediately stopped when they saw Sarah. She simply stood there, head down and motionless. She did however block the way to the stairs. The three slowly moved closer towards here, with no response. Finally in reach, Dave prodded her with the golf club, but still no response so he prodded harder.

"Are you ok?" he asked.

Sarah's head shot up to look at the three, her eyes were frenzied, her skin mottled and wrinkled, congealed blood decorated her face.

"Shit!" shouted Barry.

James stepped forward, formed a type of martial arts guard, snap kicked to her stomach, making her keel forwards, then side kicked to her face sending her tumbling onto her back, but she simply got back up and drove forwards.

"What the fuck mate, no time for kung fu, let's kill this bitch," said Dave

Dave quickly lifted up the golf club and brought it

down on to Sarah's head, but she'd lurched towards them and the club hit her with the shaft, causing it to snap in half. The golf head flew across the corridor, Dave was left holding just twenty inches of the shaft. Looking up at what he had left, it had gone quite sharp when it snapped. He changed his grip and drove the golf club into her head, but missed the eye socket as intended, driving right through her cheek and into the mouth. She still kept shambling towards the three friends.

"Mmm, fuck, shit, balls, uh, take both her arms and hold her down!" shouted Dave.

The three men were backing up at the same speed Sarah was shambling towards them. Barry and James looked at each other with amazement.

"Are you mental, mate?" said Barry.

"Stop fucking around and do it, now!" shouted Dave.

"Alright, alright," said James.

"And make sure you keep pressure on her arms to stop that jaw getting near any of us," said Dave.

The two started going forward and both grabbed at the arms, pulling her onto her back on the blood stained floor. She desperately fought to break free, but couldn't do so. Dave walked up and stood over her body, putting both hands on the golf club handle protruding from her cheek, he wrenched it from the wound. Aligning the gore covered club handle over Sarah's right eye, he shot it through the socket, driving down to the floor. Her body went instantly lifeless, blood dribbling out around the imbedded shaft.

"What a shame," said Barry.

"What?" asked Dave.

"Well she was the hottest chick in the building," said Barry.

"True," said James.

"What the fuck does that matter?" asked Dave.

"Just saying, it's a pity."

"Shut up you idiot. Right, what else can we use as weapons?"

The men walked back into their old office, Jones's still completely motionless with the monitor imbedded on his head.

"In all honesty mate, this isn't exactly the place to find weapons for fighting zombies," said James.

"So, you just want to lay down and die?" said Dave.

The men shrugged, in part understanding the sentiment, but still unable to think how any weapon could be found there. Dave tipped a desk upside down, wanting to use the legs as weapons. However, now visible was the fact that the legs were welded into the frame of the table.

There really was nothing of use in the room, the tables could not be dissembled without major power tools, the swivel office chairs didn't have any legs or useful parts that could form weapons, and everything else was fragile.

"Alright, we'll just have to try and find weapons as we go," said Dave.

The men once more edged out of their hated office for the last time. They walked towards the end of the hall towards the stairs and over the body of their latest victim. Taking the corner, they found two zombies closer to the stairs entrance than they were.

"Shite," whispered Dave.

Looking around for some useful implement, the only thing in sight was the reel of the fire hose attached to the wall. Dave grabbed this as the two creatures turned to look at them, their jaws opening at the sight of the men. Dave flicked the handle of the nozzle and the hose burst to life. Directing the water spray the creatures were pushed all the way to the back wall. The water threw them off balance, giving enough of an opening to reach the doors.

"Right, ready to run?" said Dave.

They nodded. Dave stopped the hose and all three ran for the stairway doors. The creatures were firmly on their backs from the blast, but already getting up. Fortunately, the speed that the men could run had them through the doors before the creatures were half way to them. Shutting the doors behind them they looked down, a toolbox lay on the floor. Clearly a repair man had been working there recently. Dave grabbed a bag of zip ties from the box and immediately used them to bind the door handles together. That would at least hold for long enough. He then rifled through the rest of the box. Dave passed a small crowbar to James, a long screwdriver to Barry and took a hammer in hand himself, this was the best equipped they could hope to be.

"Fucking hell, mate. This is more like it," said James.

The three men, now feeling a little safer, continued on down the enclosed stairway. Two floors down they met three zombies slowly shambling up the stairs towards them. They stopped, looked at the beasts and then each other.

"Let's fuck some shit up," said Dave.

They ran down the stairs at the three zombies. Dave hit the first one dead on the forehead with the hammer, it quivered from the blow, its skull fracturing, leaving blood seeping down its face as is tumbled back down the stairs. James swung the crowbar like a baseball bat, smacking the second one's face and causing the nose to burst, the force of the blow sending the creature tumbling back against the side wall. Before it could recover its footing, Barry leapt in front of it and drove the screw driver upwards into the eye socket and to the brain, imbedding it there permanently. Dave swung the back of the hammer around, embedding the forks in to the back of the skull of the third and final zombie, but it didn't kill it. He kicked to its stomach, lowering its head, and allowing him to lever the tool out from its skull. Finally, he twisted the hammer around and smashed it down on the nerve stem whilst the creature was still down, it immediately dropped with force to the stairs.

"Great, what do I do now?" asked Barry.

Dave handed Barry his hammer, which his friend gladly took, though rather surprised. He looked down at the hammer with a big grin, and gave it a few test swings, feeling rather happy with himself.

"Mint, mate, but what are you gonna do?"

Dave said nothing, only pointed down the stairs. The two other men looked down at what he was pointing at, and all of their eyes lit up with glee. There was a 'break in case of fire' cabinet at the next level down, just thirty feet from where they stood, and all could already make out the familiar shape of an axe inside. Dave stepped slowly and confidently down the stairs until he reached the cabinet, stopped and looked in awe at what he was about to acquire. The two men joined him, looking at the weapon lying beneath the perfectly polished glass cover.

"Barry, do the honours," said Dave.

Barry struck his hammer straight forwards and through the glass, shattering it into hundreds of little pieces. Dave reached in and took out the beast, it was a full sized, two handed fire axe, a comfortable heavy weapon. He held it up, admiring the broad, sharp edge.

"Dave, stay there a second," James said.

James backed away from the Dave whilst fumbling in his pocket.

"What are you doing?" Dave asked.

"Just getting a photo, mate," said James.

Dave chuckled, but didn't argue. He posed with the big axe whilst James snapped a picture with his iPhone. It never occurred to any of them that they would likely never get the opportunity to post the picture to Facebook. However it didn't matter, for just a few minutes they could forget about all the violence and world disaster around them, and relax.

"Right, let's move on," said Dave.

"In all honesty, mate, do you reckon we'll have space to drive on the road, even if we do get to your car?" asked Barry.

"I have no idea, but unless you just so happen to have a helicopter on the roof, it's the best idea I can think of," replied Dave.

"We need a tank," said James.

"Well go and find one then, idiot!" said Dave.

They continued on down the flight of stairs until they reached the ground floor. Dave crept up to the doors in the hallway to peer through. He looked around the open area but all was silent, he turned around to the others.

"So how are we gonna get to the car?" asked Barry.

"Right, we're going out the front and around to the car out the back, ok?"

"Why not take the back exit?" asked James.

"Because none of us have used that route, let's stick to what we know."

"Alright."

"You ready?" Dave asked.

The two men nodded.

"Right, let's go."

Dave spun around to the sight of a zombie peering through the window at him. He squealed in shock as he fell back on to the floor. The doors swung open as the creature forced its way through, it was Liam from the stores. Dave scuttled back across the floor towards his friends.

"Hit the bastard!" shouted Dave.

"But that's Liam!" replied James.

"Fuck sake!" said Dave.

Getting no assistance whatsoever from his friends, he got to his feet. Taking the axe in both hands Dave thrust the axe head towards Liam's face. The blunt heavy tip smashed into his nose and crushed it into the face, blood splashed across his already dirty flesh. The creature tumbled backwards from the force of the blow, flailing about to try and stay on its feet. Now eight yards away, Liam had regained his balance and looked up at the men, hatred in his eyes.

"Right, you're having it!"

Dave strode across through the open door towards Liam. Hoisting the axe above his head, he brought it down dead centre on Liam's cranium. The heavy axe carved through the skull and all the way to the jaw line. The skull was split in two and parted either side of the axe blade.

"Ohhh!"

Barry and James shrieked in response to the brutal display before them. The two traipsed up towards Dave. Liam's body toppled over onto its back, the axe now protruding from his head vertically. Dave put his shoe on to the parted skull and levered the blade from his victim.

"Dude that's sick, and yet, fucking cool!" said Barry.

Dave breathed out slowly with relief. All those endless days of utter boredom had built up a mass of aggression that had finally poured out in a relieving display of violence. He now revelled in his newly found vocation.

"Right, we have to get to the front doors, there will undoubtedly be more of our former colleagues on the way. They're now dead, and will do all they can do rip your heart out, so I want to see nothing but utter raw fucking violence from you, proper Scarface shit!"

The two men nodded. They looked up the hallway which would lead them to the atrium of the building. Footsteps rung out from beyond the corner and the unsettling sound of the creatures' groans followed them.

"Time to man up. Remember, strike to the head, hit hard and hit again until they drop. Now, let's get some ownage!"

The three friends strolled towards the corner of the hallway before them, moving with serious intent. The creatures appeared before them, two of the girls from reception. Dave led the attack forwards. The first zombie reached forward with both hands to try and take hold of him, but Dave smashed the axe head forwards into its stomach. It keeled over, allowing Dave to kick her in the face, knocking her off her feet. Not stopping to finish the first off, Dave continued on to the second. In one almighty horizontal cut decapitated the beast and imbedded the axe in the sidewall. The body was thrown against the wall from the force of the blow, whilst the head had already hit the ground. The remains of the beast bled down the previously clean white wall, before slowly sliding to the floor.

Dave turned around to see Barry bringing his hammer down on the zombie's head whilst she still lay flat on the floor. The strike cracked the skull, spurting blood out across the carpet, but he hit again, just to be sure. The hammer drove through the skull and imbedded into the brain. He prized the hammer head out, it was caked with brain matter.

"This is rank, mate," said Barry.

"Well it's a choice of taking or receiving," said Dave.

"Fair play," said James.

They were almost at the corner that would have them insight of the front doors of the building now, and hopefully to their escape route.

"Reception is likely to have a few bastards there, so let's keep cool and beat the shit out of them," said Dave.

The men nodded. They now set off around the corner. Taking the bend they saw the harsh reality of what they now faced. Between them and the doors were eight beasts, all of which had already turned to investigate the sounds of the three men's voices. All the creatures were people they recognised, though had never uttered more than a casual greeting to.

"This is like a free killing spree, where there's nothing to feel bad about and no police to stop you, it's like GTA for real," said Barry.

"Don't get too excited, mate, you haven't done the work yet," said Dave.

"Right, let's get to it then," said James.

James stepped forward to get first blood. The closest zombie's hands were outstretched towards him, but he beat them down with his crowbar. James then continued to hit the beast's head until the neck snapped and the head was crooked. He hit again, causing the zombie to slump lifeless to the ground.

"That's how we do things down town bitch!" said James.

Dave watched as Barry's expression grew to an enthusiastic grin, before he set off on a path of violence. Barry swung his hammer with a horizontal strike that was powerful enough to break the jaw of his first opponent. The zombie spun around and tumbled to the ground. Whilst it was still flat on the floor, he smashed his hammed down on to the nerve stem. Dave was now content that his friends were pulling their weight, so entered the fight himself.

There was not a lot of room to swing the axe now, with relatively low ceilings and his friends at his sides, so he lengthened his grip on the shaft. Reaching his first opponent, Dave smashed the front of the axe head into its knee cap, causing the leg to buckle and the beast to tumble face first to the carpet. Spinning the axe around, he struck down on the head with the back of the axe, all too aware that he couldn't risk getting the blade stuck. The large flat back smashed straight through the cavity of the skull. The beast spasmed slightly and then went still.

Barry turned to see a zombie bearing down on him, so in one move lifted the hammer from the head of his first victim and struck his second with the forks of the hammer, thoroughly embedding the tool into the zombie's head. A third came at him, but his hammer was firmly stuck. He retreated, looking for anything useful. Finally, he looked up to see a 20 inch LCD TV mounted on the wall. He took hold of it and ripped it down. Lifting the TV above his head he crashed it screen first onto his attacker's head. The glass shattered as the creature's head drove through the entire frame and out the other side. The TV was now stuck around the beast's neck like a large collar, but the zombie was still alive, despite the blood pouring from multiple gashes to its head.

"Dave!" Barry cried.

Dave ran to Barry's aid. Unable to get a good strike in, he hooked the axe head around the zombie's face from behind and then wrenched it backwards across the room. Whilst the TV collared zombie still stumbled back James took a shot at it with the crowbar. The beast's eyes went immediately lifeless as the heavy blow to the skull landed.

There were now just three zombies left before the three IT workers. Barry lifted a CO_2 fire extinguisher from one of the sidewalls and twisted the nozzle out ready to spray. He stepped forward and sprayed the extinguisher into the face of the beast, making it splutter and gurgle. Taking the opportunity presented, he took the bottle in both hands and smashed it into the zombie's skull, knocking it to the ground. He hit it again, squashing the skull to the floor.

With the axe slung over his shoulder, Dave stepped towards the next one. With the blunt end forwards he swung the tool like a baseball bat. The significant blunt trauma struck the beast's collar, immediately breaking the neck. James ran up to the last zombie, kicking upwards between its legs. The strike had almost no effect at all.

"Oh bollocks, that usually works."

The zombie's arms took hold of his shoulders, but he thrust the fork end of the crowbar upwards into its jaw. The crowbar went straight through the soft wall of the bottom of the jaw and imbedded in the upper mouth. The strike didn't stop the zombie in its tracks, who then forced James to the floor, trying to bite him, but being unable to due to the bar wedged through its mouth.

Barry kicked the side of the beast's head causing it to roll off of James. Before it could get back up he stamped five times on its face until the skull was fractured and blood expanded across the floor. Dave offered his hand out to James and helped him to his feet.

"I'm fucking knackered now," said Barry.

"Yeah, GTA was way easier than this," said James.

"Let's check the front doors," said Dave.

The three walked to the doors which were half frosted glass. The sun beaming through into the reception meant they couldn't easily see out until they got close. Arriving at them a harsh reality was unveiled. Out in the street were hundreds of creatures shambling around the town. A hundred yards in front of the building a policeman was fighting with his truncheon, surrounded by a mass of creatures. He flailed wildly about for his life, but was quickly dragged down to the ground by the horde.

"Have that you pig bastard," said Dave.

"Bit harsh, mate," said Barry.

"It's only what I saw him doing to people like us earlier this morning," replied Dave.

"Fair point," said James.

"How are we going to get out of here then?" asked Barry.

They stood at the doorway, contemplating what lay before them. It was barely halfway through the work day and they were already stuck in a world of pain.

"We need a diversion," said Dave.

"Well they aren't exactly going to follow the signs are they?" said James.

"Not that kind of diversion you idiot, something which attracts their attention away from us," said Dave.

"Got you," said James.

"Fool," said Barry.

"Oh, like you knew what he meant," said James.

"Shut up the both of you, we've got a little more to worry about that your girly fighting," said Dave.

He looked around the room. He could see a portable radio behind the reception desk.

"Sound, it's been drawing them, that's the answer."

"What?" asked Barry.

"We set up the stereo playing loud round the side of the building, and that should draw a clear path for us," said Dave.

"Alright, but we're stopping for a coffee first," said James.

"What the hell?" asked Dave.

"He's right, never leave without a coffee," said Barry.

"We're facing death every minute and you want to stay for a cuppa?" asked Dave.

"If you want us to run and fight, well then we'll need some caffeine," said James.

"Alright, fuck it, get some," said Dave.

Barry walked out to the kitchen behind the office and returned a few minutes later with three cups of coffee. The men pulled up three chairs into the middle of the reception area and sat down to relax.

"So where do we go once we've got the car?" asked Barry.

"Out of town," said Dave.

"What then?" asked James.

"Not sure, I suppose we could head out to the country."

"Why?"

"Because there'll be less zombies there," said Dave.

"We should steal a boat," said Dave.

"Like in Dawn of the Dead, that went well," said Dave.

"What about a helicopter?" asked James.

"And you know how to fly it?" said Dave.

The three men fell silent, each trying to think of a better solution once they were free of the current threat. Not a single one they could think of was particularly favourable.

"Let's face it. If we stay here we're dead. So let's get away from places with lots of people and not worry about what to do if we make it," said Dave.

The two others nodded in agreement, though neither was particularly satisfied with that. The three colleagues sat for five minutes drinking their coffees without saying a word to each other. The sound and groans of the horde outside was ever present, as was the odd siren in the distance. A short cry in pain or fear could be heard now and again around the street, yet more people overcome by the masses of blood thirsty creatures.

"That's time enough, drink up, we're moving out," said Dave.

The two friends miserably downed what was left of their coffees and got to their feet with zero enthusiasm. Barry went over to the lifeless zombie with his hammer still stuck out of its head, and prised it out. James picked up his crowbar and Dave his newly acquired radio.

"I'm going to set this up round the side of the building in an open window. As soon as the music is pounding I'll be back, and we'll out of here at the first opening," said Dave.

He wandered out of the room with the radio in hand. Finding the window as far away as possible from the front doors he plugged the radio back in. The windows, being as they were security windows would only open a few inches, but it was enough to have the desired effect. Dave flicked the radio on and turned it up full, it was time to run!

Back in reception, Barry and James could already see the zombies' attention turn to the new sound echoing from around the side of the building. Dave got back to the room to see a large number of the creatures shambling towards it. The worst of the horde was rapidly moving from harm's way, but the opening would not last long.

"You ready to run?" asked Dave.

He pulled the doors open, light piercing the dim and

dusky building. A disgusting smell wafted through the opening, a combination of various things burning and dying. The three men made a break from the building. The car was just five hundred yards around the corner, on the first floor of a small multi-storey car park.

They were keeping up a steady jog towards the getaway car, weaving in between the few creatures that had resisted the urge to be drawn to Dave's diversion. As they ran between three creatures, Barry swung his hammer without stopping sending a zombie spinning around in a blood stained mess to the floor. The men reached the street where the car was parked, now just a hundred yards away and in sight. Four creatures blocked their path.

"Almost there lads, let's not fuck this up now," said Dave.

The three moved quickly towards the parked car. Dave led the way, Barry soon behind with James at the rear. Now with the room to swing Dave lifted his axe overhead and swung it down at the first creature's head. The blow just missed the beast's head and impeded in the collar bone causing it to crumble at the knees from the force. The beast still hissed with hatred, despite being barely able to move. Holding onto the shaft, Dave kicked the creature in the face, throwing it back and off the blade. He reversed his grip and used the axe head like a slide hammer, smashing down on the beast's nose, flattening it.

As Dave and Barry turned their attentions to the last

two creatures before them and the car, James stood next to a tall brick wall, not knowing what to do with himself. He was suddenly knocked to the ground by a body landing on him. A zombie had tumbled over from the brick wall. James knocked his head on the tarmac as he landed, and the beast was on him. It bit deep in to his throat and ripped a large part from his flesh.

The two friends looked back to see the zombie on their friend. His hands were cupped around his neck, blood poured from his wound in an ever expanding puddle around his body. Dave rushed back and swung his axe with a big horizontal blow. The creature looked up at Dave running at it, snarling at him, but the large blunt back edge of the weapon struck it square in the face, knocking it off James.

"James, James, hang in there!"

Dave put pressure down on the wound but blood continued to spew from between both their fingers. James gargled as he was choking on his own blood. Barry looked on at the desperate situation, but was suddenly all too aware of the moans of two beasts bearing down on them. He spun to see the first just a few feet from him. Now feeling utter hatred for the disgusting creatures that had injured his friend, he lifted the crowbar to his shoulder like a baseball bat. Barry smashed the crowbar down on the creature's head, causing it to lose its balance. He did not allow it time to recover, striking again, hitting the shoulder, then again to the neck, until finally a heavy strike down onto the skull. The zombie's skull opened as blood spewed out on to the street.

Not stopping to witness his handy work, Barry ran at the last one just ten feet in front of him. He swung the crowbar into its stomach causing it to keel over, then cracking the bar down onto the back of its exposed neck. The beast slammed to the tarmac, face downwards, but Barry kept hitting. The skull was obliterated by multiple beatings that Barry's frenzy caused. He finally stopped when the creature's head was as flat as the street it lay on.

Walking back over to his two friends, Barry could see that James was fighting for the last breaths in his life. But Dave was unwilling to give up. James was now gasping heavily and had lost more blood than anyone could expect to survive.

"Mate," said Barry.

Dave ignored him.

"Dave!" shouted Barry.

"What?" Dave snarled back.

"You know what we have to do," said Barry.

"No, not James," said Dave.

Barry grabbed Dave by the shoulders and pulled him from their dying friend. Dave stumbled back, but before he could regain his footing, Barry stepped between him and James, holding him back.

"What do you think is going to happen here? He's

gone!" shouted Barry.

"So you're just going to leave him to die by himself?" asked Dave.

"What else is there to do?" said Barry.

Dave calmed himself slightly, common sense and reality finally kicking in. He released his pressure and Barry stepped aside. They both looked over at James, he was now completely motionless, having breathed his last breath. The two men simply stood, pale faced, looking at their dead friend. This wasn't all the fun the movies led you to believe. After just a few seconds his eyes re-opened, and he sat up.

"It's time to end this, he isn't our friend anymore," said Barry.

Dave, now having got past the worst of his emotions and back to his practical self, lifted his axe on to his shoulder. Before James had time to rise from the seated position on the pavement, Dave's axe was descending on him. The axe struck dead centre on the skull and provided a quick death to their old friend. Dave sorrowfully put his shoe on to his friend's dead body and prized the blade from his skull.

"Let's get out of this hell hole," said Dave.

"Agreed," said Barry.

The two men moved towards Dave's car, his most prized position. The car was a 2002 Honda Civic Type R, black with gunmetal wheels. It was an evil looking car, and was soon to be put to good use. The two put their weapons in through to the back seat and jumped in, strapping into the four point harnesses. Turning the key the V-Tech engine roared to life, the best sound they'd heard all day.

"It's going to be a rough ride out of town, this is perhaps the one day I wish I'd bought a Land Rover," said Dave.

"At least you own a car, mate," said Barry.

"True, you tight bastard," said Dave.

He revved the engine and slipped the clutch, burning the front tyres as they launched onto the street. Reaching the main road it was more like an obstacle course than the straight road they were familiar with.

Dodging an upturned police car, the Civic raced between the endless scatterings of creatures. Taking a blind bend Dave clipped one of the zombies with the front wing, sending it tumbling into a wall. Keeping the speed up they were coming to an intersection. A mass of creatures were approaching from the way they were heading. At the crossroads Dave yanked the handbrake upwards and spun the car to the right side, slamming into the mass of creatures with the side of his car, knocking them backwards. Putting the power down they were again steaming ahead.

"To think I only washed the car on Saturday, what a shame," said Dave.

A few hundred yards ahead an ambulance flew across an intersection, striking four zombies that were staggering across the road. The bodies of the creatures were thrown across the street. Slightly out of control the ambulance struck a bollard and tumbled onto its side, scraping and sliding across the pavement until it smashed through a shop front.

"Don't stop, there's nothing we can do for them," said Barry.

"Agreed," said Dave.

The two tore through the streets, deserted in many parts, zombies scattered in varying quantities in others. They were now getting clearer of the inner city limits and really opening up the throttle, racing through thirty miles per hour limits at eighty. "This is the best I've felt all day," said Dave.

"Without a doubt, mate," said Barry.

Up ahead a lorry was parked across much of the road. Dave didn't even slow down, feeling confident from his track experience, and using the taut steering to quickly manoeuvre around the obstacle. As he came out from the bend it became clear that a body lay in the road.

"Shit!" shouted Dave.

The right front quarter struck the body, jolting the car. The tyre burst and the car pulled quickly over, crashing in to a parked saloon. A few moments later the two men came back to consciousness, the air bags having momentarily dazed them. Barry reeled in pain. Dave looked over to him, not seeing how he would have been injured whilst being in the harness. Then it became clear, the side of the car was buckled inwards, crushing his left leg and hip. The car had struck the saloon square on the passenger door and then bounced off onto a pavement, tumbling bonnet first into a post box, which is where they now sat, in plain sight.

"Fuck me, mate, that was rubbish," said Barry.

"Tell me about it," replied Dave.

Dave looked around, all was silent, the engine having stalled and nobody in sight. He reached for the ignition, the engine turned over, but nothing else happened. He tried again, and a third time, but nothing.

"Bugger," said Dave.

All was looking hopeless. The two simply sat back, losing the will to live.

"Look," said Barry.

He was pointing through his window down the road. About half a mile away the familiar shape of the shambling dead could be seen making their way towards the car.

"Great, that's all we need," said Dave.

He got out of the car and pulled his axe from the back seat. Walking over to the passenger side, Barry had not got out.

"Is the door jammed, mate?" asked Dave.

"Yeh," he replied.

Dave put his hand onto the door handle and lifted, but nothing happened. Putting more pressure it would still not move.

"Hang on, mate."

Dave walked back around the car and climbed in the back to find Barry's hammer. Looking over his friend's shoulder he could see a blood trail, not a good sign.

Dave walked back around to the passenger side and slipped the hammer forks in between the door frame and car. Prizing the two apart he did all he could do get the door open. The metal of the body buckled, but the door showed no sign of moving.

"Fuck!" he shouted.

"Mate, get me the fuck out of here!" shouted Barry.

He hammered on the door frame, as much in anger as desperation. Barry was panicking. Finally, he stopped, already tired, and having achieved nothing at all. Dave leant against the car, knowing nothing else to do that might help, and seeing the zombies getting closer.

"Mate, I'm done," said Barry.

"What do you mean?" asked Dave.

"I'm stuck here, and even if you could get that door open, I doubt I could walk, my leg is mangled, and my hip wrecked," said Barry.

"So what?" asked Dave.

"So, you can do me the courtesy of not leaving me to become one of those things," said Barry

"What?" asked Dave.

"You're free to run, and you should. I'm not, I would

rather be killed by a friend than a zombie," said Barry.

"No fucking way, mate," said Dave.

"Then what, you'd rather leave me to bleed out and become one of those things?"

Dave stopped to think. It was a horrible situation, and the hardest decision he'd ever made in his life. The day had started in a rubbish fashion, but what was a boring office life seemed all too comfortable when faced with this.

"What do you want me to do?" asked Dave.

"You have to kill me in the same way we killed the others, so that there's no way for me to become one of them," said Barry.

"Like how?" asked Dave.

"Take that hammer, and hit me on the noggin with it, hard," said Barry.

"Jesus, mate, I can't do that," said Dave.

"Man the fuck up, you'll be doing me a favour," said Barry.

"Well it doesn't feel like it," said Dave.

"It's been an interesting day, but it's now time you got moving, now please, do it and go," said Barry.

Dave picked the hammer up, it was still stained with the blood of several creatures. In his head this was the worst thing he would ever do, but in his heart he knew it was also the kindest.

"See ya, mate," said Dave.

"Yeah, in heaven, I'll be waiting there at the nearest bar."

"Ha, sounds good."

Dave faced away from his friend and quickly swung the hammer in horizontally at his head, striking the temple hard. Barry was killed instantly, but Dave didn't look back to see the result of his work. He looked up, a scattering of creatures were enthusiastically stumbling towards him, now just a hundred yards away. Looking over at the side of a road, a bicycle was chained to the railings outside a newsagent.

A bike would be the last mode of transport Dave would ever choose to use, but he only had to keep a mild speed up to be free of these beasts, and there was no time to find anything else. With both weapons in hand he ran over to the bike. Looking down it, it was a nice new mountain bike and locked with a steel chain. The door beside him suddenly swung open and Dave turned just in time to see the zombified storekeeper staggering towards him, finally something to take his anger out on. He put the axe loose in his left hand and took Barry's hammer up with his right. Swinging at the man the first blow hit the nose, causing it to erupt in blood. Before the creature could recover he hit again, the hammer head smashing into the eye socket and forcing the eyeball out loose, dangling from the beast's face.

Dave pulled the hammer from the socket and slammed

it down on to the beast's forehead, splintering the skull. Blood dripped down the creature's mangled face, but it was still not dead. He lifted the hammer again and swung it down onto the beast's head again and again, until it dropped in a lifeless mess.

Looking out across the wall of the shop, Dave could see a number of creatures getting ever closer. He took the hammer to the chain, but it wouldn't break. He took the axe and stood up. Raising it over his head he smashed it down on the lock, but still no result. Dave hit it again and again, until finally on the sixth strike the lock partly broke. He wedged the forks of the hammer between what was left of the lock and prized them apart. Unfortunately, Dave could no longer carry his beloved axe, as there was no means to do so on a bicycle. He took the hammer and jumped onto the bike. It was a bleak continuation from a journey which should have included both his two friends and treasured Type R.

As he rode off from the shop front pavement a creature took the turn around the wall ahead of him. Dave could have avoided this creature, but the absolute hatred he now felt for the beasts made him deliberately veer closer. Riding past leisurely to the left side of the zombie he smacked it hard in the face. The beast's neck twisted sharply and it collapsed to the street. He continued on. The relaxed fighting position and ride afforded him a comfortable journey out of the town, and the revenge he so desperately wanted could be had at any moment he chose. Every hundred yards, Dave would hammer another zombie in the face, each time feeling just a little better about things than he had before.

Finally, he reached a small bridge which crossed over the motorway. Getting to the railings he stopped to look below. The road was always busy, no matter the time or day, but now the traffic was stopped completely, but there were few people. Some creatures could be seen hammering on windows and staggering between the jam. However many people survived in those cars, they would not for long, and there was nothing Dave could do about it.

Looking back from where he'd just come two creatures staggered towards him in the distance. The only way was forwards. Dave was now quickly growing tired, he had the willpower to ride on, but little else. He followed the road to a village he'd never heard of, it would at least have as few people as possible, less potential enemies. Time was going on, with just a few hours of light, he only hoped he could find shelter before this terrible day was over.

CHAPTER SEVEN

Helmand Province, Afghanistan

It was Afghanistan and even though it was only 5am the marines were already feeling the start of the day's heat. Though they'd been in the country for three months now, none of them enjoyed being out in full combat gear in the blistering temperature. The country was dry, barren and the dust and sand got everywhere. On top of this they were crammed in like sardines into the Osprey, an aircraft that on paper was state-of-the-art, but to the marines it was like every other vehicle they travelled in; noisy, dark and cramped!

Each of the marines was equipped with the latest Modular Tactical Vest (MTV) set of body armour which was the newest and most advanced vest in marine inventories. It offered better protection than previous vests and was proving invaluable in the continuing war with the insurgency. The marines also wore the latest Combat Utility Uniform that consisted of MARPAT digital camouflage blouse and trousers, green undershirt, and tan suede boots. On their heads they wore the new Lightweight Helmets that offered better protection than the previous 'Fritz' type designs even though they were less than light! These marines looked well armed and equipped and were the spearhead of the US Marines assault troops.

Reports had been coming in all morning and the stories were not good, not good at all. Private Torres, a twenty four year old marine tried to find out more as he read the latest on his Apple iPhone. He was taller than average, shaved hair and was the stereotypical jarhead. He squinted as he tried to examine the small scrolling ticker at the bottom. The tiny text gave him the latest figures whilst on the main screen he was watching a live video feed.

He turned to the man sat next to him and thrust the phone at his face. Making sure that the display was placed right in front of his nose.

"Have you seen this shit?" he asked excitedly. "The attacks are spreading!"

The man ignored the phone and swore directly as Torres.

"Get that piece of shit out of my face!"

The other men onboard laughed at the usual banter

between these two men. Torres was always waving his phone about, much to the annoyance of the rest who were convinced he must work for the company. Torres pretended to not have heard his comments and described what he had read.

"According to this report some of those guys managed to attack the English parliament."

Fernanda, the unit's only female soldier leaned forwards, looking towards Torres. She had short, dark hair tied loose behind her head and carried her M4 carbine across her chest.

"How many this time?" she shouted.

Torres examined the screen more closely, watching the video feed of the action. Though the footage was small he could see the inside of the building, incredibly the panic had been caught on camera. As armed police arrived, firing automatic weapons, the feed started to stutter and parts of the video froze.

"I'm losing the signal. I think it said the Prime Minister was injured and there are more than fifty more dead or injured. They said something about martial law I think," said Torres.

Fernanda leaned back, "First Canada gets hit, then France. When is this gonna stop?"

The rest of the men were silent. They were all experienced marines from the 3rd Battalion, 4th Marines infantry battalion of the United States Marine Corps.

Known by the rest of the armed forces as the 'Thundering Third', they had already accumulated an impressive score of victories in the country. Unlike their previous missions though, this was only their third in the new Osprey aircraft. They were sat inside the V22-Osprey and it was cramped, especially with the rest of the unit packed in. This aircraft was the latest piece of equipment in the arsenal of the US Marines and over time it would be replacing most of the battlefield helicopters. It was a tiltrotor aircraft with both a vertical takeoff and landing capability, and combined the functionality of a conventional helicopter with the long-range, high-speed cruise performance of a fixed wing aircraft.

The First Sergeant, a tough marine called Black was standing up, holding onto one of the internal rails whilst he spoke over the headset to the pilots. Something caught his attention and he moved closer to the front of the aircraft, engaging in a conversation for about a minute. The rest of the marines tried to hear what was going on. It didn't matter though because after just a few more seconds he moved to the centre of the aircraft and tapped his ear, signalling to the men to fit their intercom systems on so they could be more easily heard over the sound of the two massive rotors.

"Ok ladies, listen up. We've received reports from Nawzad District that the operation has hit a shit storm," he said.

Now that he had their attention he continued.

"The ANA units patrolling the Nawzad Valley were hit earlier this morning. Information from our Force Recon unit there says they've been wiped out and Nawzad itself has been hit by Taliban forces. That was an hour ago, since then we've heard nothing."

The Sergeant looked around the craft, spotting the concern and anger amongst the men. He received more information and gestured to the marines to wait whilst he listened in.

Sergeant Black had been involved in operations in Nawzad three months earlier and he was dismayed to hear that this success story seemed to be unravelling. Though not particularly massive it was the centre of the Nawzad District in Helmand Province. The area had been fought over for the last few years by the Taliban forces on one side and the outnumbered British forces with their Ghurkha troops and small numbers of the new Afghan National Army soldiers. Though they'd fought hard their numbers just weren't enough to do the job alone. With the heavy fighting over in Iraq they'd been able to transfer combat forces, including the Marine units, to Helmand Province to assist their comrades in the British Army. With the skills and knowledge of the area the British were capable allies and the process of pacifying the region was now coming to an end.

He stopped, listening to more news on his headset

before continuing.

"We have the latest intel from the Reapers, it shows the area has been involved in some kind of action but there are no signs of insurgents moving in the area.

"Any news on the garrison in the town?" asked Torres.

"Not since the start of the action. At 4.25am we received news that the civilians were being attacked and shortly after that the two compounds came under fire. All transmissions stopped at 4.42am and we have to assume that Coalition and ANA forces in the town have been neutralised. This area is critical to our progress in the Nawzad Valley."

The Sergeant spoke a few words into his headset before turning back to Torres.

"Remember marines, we're here to disrupt Taliban supply and communications lines and to remove his support in this region."

He lifted himself up straight, looking at the rest of the marines in the Osprey.

"Either way we need to retake control and bring this town back under the control of the ANA," said the sergeant.

Lieutenant Wade, a pale looking officer, moved from the cockpit into the main passenger area. He thrust a map into Sergeant Black's hands and shouted into the sergeant's ear. He looked at it for a moment before nodding and passing the map back to him, saying a few words. The

Lieutenant moved back to the front of the craft, avoiding eye contact with the rest of the marines.

Sergeant Black continued his explanation to the men.

"The plan has changed, we're no longer on a logistical mission, this is now a combat operation and you will hit the ground running. Make sure your gear is ready, we hit the ground in sixty seconds!"

A chorus of 'Ooh-rah' echoed through the noisy interior. The marines grabbed their weapons, each checking their ammunition and equipment. The marines, as always were well equipped for most tasks. Between them they carried a significant amount of rifles and machineguns, as well as grenade launcher attachments and grenades. There was little they couldn't handle. The First Sergeant continued.

"We'll be landing half a click from the south of the town. Our mission is to secure the main access to the town from the south and then to hump down to the forward base and establish a foothold. Once we've taken it we'll evacuate any wounded and reinforce the position prior to the arrival of additional ANA units," said Sergeant Black.

The interior warning lights came on, indicating that the unit would be landing shortly. The massive engines on the short, stubby wings groaned as they changed position. The rotors were currently forward facing, just like the engines in an aircraft like a C130 Hercules. As the motors moved though they changed configuration until the V22 looked more like a conventional helicopter.

From the small window Torres could see the dusty ground as the aircraft swooped down in its standard landing pattern. This procedure was the most dangerous part of their trip as they were slower and most vulnerable as they lowered down to the ground. Unlike other aircraft such as helicopters the Osprey used a more automated landing procedure that made touchdown more predictable. On top of this the Osprey needed much more space than an equivalent helicopter to land, making potential landing zones more obvious to the enemy. The end result was that the marines wanted to get out as quickly as possible.

As the ground rushed upwards, Torres found his visibility was ruined by a huge cloud of dust. This was one problem that so far hadn't been solved. Because of the two massive rotors and the immense downdraft the V-22 Osprey created a huge dust cloud that surrounded the craft upon landing. This was known as brownout and was the problem responsible for three out of four helicopter crashes and losses in Afghanistan. The downside was that the men could see almost nothing upon leaving, the upside was that it created a smokescreen for their arrival.

With a thud the Osprey hit the ground, sliding a few feet forwards, the undercarriage compressed, taking the impact on the hard, dry soil and cushioning the landing. In seconds the tail ramp dropped down, exposing the men to the elements. Lowering his goggles the Sergeant was the first out, signalling to the rest of the men to follow him. It didn't take long, none of the marines wanted to stay a moment longer in a lightly armoured aircraft that was kicking up a cloud that could be seen for miles in every direction. As the men left the Osprey they moved back about thirty metres to take cover behind the rocks and cover nearby. The aircraft took off almost as soon as the last man left. The downdraft was massive and blew sand and dust over the men as they sheltered.

The second Osprey came in low, looking like a futuristic drop ship from a science fiction movie. It hit the ground and quickly disgorged its marines nearby giving a total of forty two men, a full, combat ready Marine rifle platoon. The platoon consisted of three rifle squads each led by a sergeant. With single hand signal the three NCO's responded to First Lieutenant Wade and split up, the three squads moving out to secure the landing area. The unit was a short distance from the town, a slightly raised position within the remnants of a few low broken walls and barbed wire marking the perimeter. In the previous campaigns this had actually been a forward base, now it was simply a convenient resupply position that usually housed a handful of ANA soldiers. As the marines spread out it was clear that it was missing any sign of the soldiers. Near the northern perimeter was a small blockhouse that was used as a shelter for the guards. The 1st Squad was already in position and in sections stormed the room and the area around it to find the place deserted. Sergeant

Weathers moved in first, followed by one of his riflemen. There was a sound of equipment being kicked around before he returned, moving up to the Lieutenant.

"Sir, no sign of them. Their weapons are still here and the communication equipment is on, but not transmitting," he said.

Lieutenant Wade signalled to the leaders of the other two squads, calling them over.

"Ok, uh, I want 1st Squad to stay here with me," he looked around at what was left of the compound, "we need to make this defensible in case of any attempt to re-take it."

Sergeants Black and Weathers exchanged knowing looks. Their confidence in the officer was at an all time low. Luckily the Marine Corps placed great emphasis on its NCO's and their ability to command. This was something that had been a tradition right back to the island hopping campaigns in the Pacific back in World War II.

The Lieutenant, looking nervous continued with his orders, looking first at Sergeant Black.

"We need to secure this point and co-ordinate the relief of the town."

He waved his arm, pointing at the abandoned base.

"Weathers, I want 1st Squad to setup a defensive perimeter around this LZ. Get the heavy weapons set up and establish a command post in there," he pointed to the small blockhouse.

The sergeant saluted and then moved back, shouting out to his men. In just seconds the men from 1st Squad were busy preparing the position. Lieutenant Wade seemed to forget what he was doing for a moment, looking around the old site. Whatever he was thinking, it certainly wasn't inspiring confidence in the men. Sergeant Black stepped closer, drawing attention to himself.

"Sir!" he called.

The Lieutenant turned back to face the NCO, the realisation that he needed to do more than just dig a hole and hide possibly kicking in. Wade paused and then seemed to regain his composure.

"Sergeant Black, I want you take 2nd Squad and advance to the bazaar. I need to know what has happened in the town," he said.

Sergeant Black looked confused.

"What about 3rd Squad, Sir? I could do with the manpower. We've got no intel on the area and no idea what might be there," he said.

He tried to make it sound like a suggestion rather than the obvious way it should be done, but it was difficult for him to hide the derision he had for the officer. It was his job to keep his marines alive and combat ready.

"I'm sure it's nothing you can't handle, Sergeant. Get to it! I've got other things to do."

Mathews, an experienced NCO in his own right interrupted.

"I agree with Sergeant Black, Sir. Sending just one squad into the bazaar could be risky. If we send in..."

He was stopped by Wade raising his hand.

"Look, I have a job for 3rd Squad. Just get your men ready and tell me when you've secured the bazaar."

He turned away, an obvious signal that he'd finished his discussion with the men. Sergeant Black saluted and then turned to his men to get them ready.

"I have a special mission for you Mathews. Apparently the last reports said something about fighting near the supply compound here," said Wade.

He pointed to his map, showing him the location of the site that appeared about half way into the town and probably five hundred metres from the bazaar.

The sergeant scratched his chin in confusion.

"I don't understand, Sir. The bazaar is not far away, wouldn't it be more efficient to secure the compound first with 2nd Squad and then sweep into the bazaar once we have a central position to operate from," he said, almost pleading.

"No, Sergeant, that is not helpful. We're marines and I want both objectives taken before the rest of the unit arrives. This is our mission and we deserve the credit for securing the town."

"But Sir, it's not a race, my men..." he said.

"Sergeant! You will secure the compound and keep me informed, that is all!" he shouted.

Sergeant Mathews saluted, knowing full well that the discussion was over and that this mission had just taken a deadly turn for the worse. He spotted Sergeant Black about to leave and made his way discretely over to the man. Black spotted him and paused for a moment, so they could speak.

"This is shit," said Black, "I'm not sending my men into an ambush. Wade is an assfuck!"

Mathews smiled, "I agree. He wants me to take the compound first."

Sergeant Black examined his map. He traced two lines with hands, leading from their landing zone and out to the two objectives.

"I don't understand this, we could easily support each other and take both locations, one after the other," he said.

Sergeant Mathews considered the situation. He looked around, noticing the Lieutenant was already chasing the men of 1st Squad to set up his base of operations. He'd come up with a simple solution.

"Wade is too busy building his little empire here, I suggest we split up as ordered, but I'll radio in that the route is blocked," he suggested.

Black knew exactly what he was getting at, "Yeah, then you can move through these alleys and will be forced to take the same route as us."

"Exactly," answered Mathews, "we'll still be following orders and the mission is still the same."

"Same, apart from it not being a shit plan!" said Black grinning.

"Let's do this!"

The two squads moved out from the compound and down the hill. They made a special effort to maintain two separate columns, one for each of the squads as they entered the outer suburbs of the town.

Nawzad was a small town of probably ten thousand inhabitants. Most had fled after the fighting between the Taliban and the British sometime before. Since the marines had provided extra manpower they had forced the enemy out and life was slowly returning to the place. It was still much more sparsely populated than before, intelligence suggested that no more than four thousand people remained. The town itself consisted of a well known bazaar that was used by many of the outlying towns and villages. Through the centre ran the main road, and a maze of mud-brick houses and compounds, interspersed with narrow alleys. It was hardly a thriving metropolis, but in the new Afghanistan it was a start, and it was their job to make it stay that way.

Through this main street moved 2nd Squad. Sergeant Black had split the three fire teams across the street with half of the men moving down what he would consider the sidewalks, keeping close to the low buildings and looking for any potential threats. Experience had shown him that moving out in the open in this country made you both easy to spot and also easy to shoot at.

Overhead the sound of the two Ospreys could be heard. They were heading away and with them gone they had no immediate way to leave the place or to move quickly. Black thought to himself that Wade had better not have fucked them over.

"We're on the main highway, so far no hostiles spotted. Route is clear, over," he whispered into the headset.

The Ospreys were now both clear of the men and started their return trip to collect more men and supplies for the operation. With the craft moving away the visibility down the main street improved.

As the squad moved into the outskirts of the town they were surprised to see it looking very different to the reconnaissance photographs they'd studied the night before. Rather than being the bustling small town in the images it looked instead as though there had been a small war fought in the last few hours. The main street was littered with vehicles, some of them crashed, others abandoned and some still burning. What was even worse though was the amount of bodies.

"The situation is not good. There are bodies everywhere, looks like there's been major action. Over," he said, listening for a response.

"Sir, I advise we get aerial reconnaissance ASAP. We need to know what's ahead. Based on the number of bodies something big happened here," he said.

There was a pause before the voice of a frustrated Wade appeared in his ear.

"Sergeant, I'm not interested in a few bodies. This is Afghanistan, it's always the same. Stop dawdling and get to the bazaar!" said the annoying voice on the radio.

"Understood," replied Black.

He threw down his hand in resignation and then continued down the road. He swore to himself, his indignation at being spoken to like a child was bad enough, but in this country these kinds of petty arguments costs his squad lives. After moving a few more blocks ahead he stopped at the worst scene of carnage so far. A small truck had been abandoned in the middle of a crossroads and around it were crashed cars and bodies. It looked as though there had been some kind of battle in this part of the town, especially where the vehicles were, groups of bodies were formed up almost like a large circle.

Torres spoke quietly to the Sergeant, "You know what this reminds me of?"

Sergeant Black moved around one of the cars, examining the bodies thrown up against it.

"What's that Torres?" he asked.

"It looks like one of those fifties films, you know the ones where the Ancients were fighting with swords. Look at the bodies, it's like a last stand or something," said Torres.

Sergeant Black scanned the area, it was weird, but Torres

might be onto something. The bodies were strange, it did look like they'd been killed trying to defend a position in the street. Then it dawned on him.

"Fuck. It's a barricade!" he called.

Torres thought he heard something and moved off to the right, checking under the truck whilst Fernanda climbed up the side and looked inside, spotting bodies.

"Sir!" she called.

Sergeant Black moved up and called over, "What is it, Corporal?"

"We've got a survivor here, Sir. It looks like he's injured."

Black didn't bother climbing up, he had plenty of carnage to see and simply nodded to the marine.

"Get him out. We need to keep on to the compound. I don't want to stay out here any longer than necessary. Some weird shit is going on and we need to be somewhere else."

Corporal Fernanda nodded and looked inside, checking the door for signs of tampering or bombs. After two tours in Afghanistan she was well experienced in the kind of sick improvised explosive devices that the insurgents used against them. It all looked clear. Keeping her weapon ready she pulled at the door with her left hand. It swung open to reveal the injured man inside. She turned and called down.

"Bush and Anders, get your asses up here and give me

a hand to get this guy out.

Black interrupted, "The rest of you secure the crossroads. We're not far from the bazaar now."

As they pulled out the wounded local the rest of the troops moved a short distance ahead, making their way cautiously past the bodies and vehicles. There was still no sign of any survivors. Whoever had attacked them had been highly efficient at leaving no witnesses. The fireteam to the right found their progress blocked by a trailer that had been dumped, almost as though the owner had wanted to cause a problem. It blocked off part of the road and the entire sidewalk. That was not what stopped them though, it was the sight of the crashed Humvee. A quick examination showed that there were no bodies nearby. Corporal Atkins appeared from behind the vehicle.

"Looks like enemy action to me. The tyres are blown out and the offside wheel is missing, I think from an IED," he said.

The High Mobility Multipurpose Wheeled Vehicle, or Humvee, was a large military four-wheel drive vehicle that had largely supplanted the roles formerly served by smaller Jeeps and other light trucks. It was versatile, tough and could be modified for a variety of combat roles and was a very common sight in Afghanistan. Over 10,000 alone were employed by coalition forces during Operation Iraqi Freedom, the 2003 invasion of Iraq.

Sergeant Black arrived on the scene, confused by the

lack of survivors.

"Could they be back at the compound?" he asked.

The man shrugged, "Maybe, it's where I would be right now if this shit was going, Sarge."

The Sergeant thought for just a moment before signalling for the squad to keep moving on. He pulled the mic closer to his mouth.

"Team Charlie, this is Team Bravo. What is your situation?" he said.

There was a slight pause before the familiar voice of Sergeant Mathews from 3rd Squad came back to him.

"Black, we've found some major shit here. There are bodies in the ally and we're making slow progress. Wait, there's something strange about this body," said Mathews.

"Same here, it looks like the main street was blocked off for a firefight. We're continuing on to the target area. What about the body?" asked Black.

Before he could say anymore a screech came down the radio followed by shouting. Then the radio went dead. He called back into the mic, receiving nothing. Then came the gunfire, but not through the radio, he could hear it coming from the alleys off towards where 3rd Squad must be.

Atkins climbed up onto one of the cars for a better view. He called over to the sergeant.

"Sarge, I can hear Kalashnikovs, it must be the Taliban," he said.

"Maybe," muttered Black as he tapped his mic.

"Base control, this is Team Bravo. We have shots fire from the direction of Team Charlie. Request change in command, we need to provide extraction, over."

"That's a negative Bravo, proceed to the bazaar, do not wait. That is an order," came the reply.

"What the fuck?" shouted Black off the radio.

He turned back to his squad but before he could give his orders Jones shouted out.

"Sarge, look!"

The Sergeant looked in the direction the soldier was pointing at to reveal a group of about thirty people emerging from far away in the distance, possibly four to five hundred metres away. With his training kicking in, Sergeant Black ducked down behind the nearest abandoned car, the rest of the men did the same. He checked his M4 carbine and then lifted himself up slowly, watching the group who were only a short distance away.

Anders called over to him, "Sarge, there's something wrong with this guy, look!"

The Sergeant moved over, keeping low to avoid the attention of the group near the tanker. As he came closer to the wounded man he could see that his face was white as a sheet and his breathing was almost non-existent. What worried him much more though was the thick blood dripping down from the corner of his mouth. The first thought that occurred to him was that this looked like a biological or chemical attack or poison.

"Shit, get back from him!" he shouted.

The Sergeant's timing couldn't have been better, as soon as Anders stepped back the man coughed, spurting out a mouthful of foul blood before falling back down. Anders moved a little closer, putting his fingers onto the man's throat to feel for a pulse. He paused for a moment, trying to get a solid reading.

"Shit, Sarge, I'm not getting a pulse!" he cried.

A series of groans and cries came from the direction of the crowd shambling down the street. Though they were a good distance away they were in the exact direction the marines needed to go. Private Bennett, who was sheltering behind a car, lifted up his M249 machinegun and placed it on the roof of the abandoned Corolla. He shouted over to the Sergeant.

"Hey, Sarge. They look like fucking zombies to me, man!"

Sergeant Black took just three steps to reach the marine and immediately interrupted the man, putting his hand on his shoulder and spinning him around. The soldier, who until now had almost been enjoying watching down the street started to panic until he spotted the Sergeant. His panic simply increased when the hulk of the man started to shout down his throat.

"Watch that shit, Private!" he barked.

The private acknowledged, returned to his weapon,

somewhat chastened. He pulled back the cocking handle, preparing for possible action. The M249 light machine gun was an American version of the Belgian FN Minimi, and provided infantry squads with the heavy volume of fire of a machine gun combined with accuracy and portability approaching that of a rifle.

The large group of shambling civilians continued their slow progress down the street, moving between the abandoned cars and towards the soldiers. At this rate they would probably take at least five minutes, maybe longer to reach them.

Sergeant Black wasn't happy, he'd heard of similar situations before. It didn't take long for a situation like this to turn into a fully fledged firefight with an enemy that knew the ground, had prepared positions and potentially placed IEDs. He called out to the unit leaders.

"First fireteam take the left, second with me in the street and third watch that truck."

The marines moved to get into better positions, keeping as little of their bodies exposed to what could be the enemy. The biggest problems were the units on the flanks. The squad on the left flank was exposed as they were halfway though moving across the street. They pulled back, taking up positions around the larger corner building on the crossroads. On the right Atkins and his men took cover around the crashed tanker and the Humvee.

Anders called out something from the position of the

dead man from the truck, whilst Sergeant Black called in their progress with his radioman. He moved back to see what the problem was. From what he could see, the dead man was sitting up, yet his face still had the look of a dead man.

Out on the right flank Atkins signalled that he'd seen movement on the rooftop of the buildings to their right.

"Sarge, I think they might be trying to flank us!" he called out.

"Shit!" swore Black. He signalled towards Atkins. With the acknowledgement from Sergeant Black, Atkins sent in the fireteam to clear the building. The fireteam was made up of four marines, the team leader with an M4 carbine, one rifleman with another M4, one grenadier and one light machine gunner with the teams M249 machinegun. The grenadier was armed the same as a rifleman, apart from the fact that he had a grenade launcher fitted to his rifle.

The team leader, Lance Corporal Winchester moved up to the door whilst the other three provided cover in case of attack. Winchester crept slowly forward ever wary of wire or buried explosives. The door looked clear but who knew what was on the other side. He turned to check on his men, they were ready. With one swift kick he smashed open the door and the grenadier and riflemen both rushed in, taking up positions on each side of the door of the building.

As the rest of the men entered the room they were all

relived to find no hostiles or booby traps, not yet anyway. The room was quite small and looked like it hadn't been lived in for a while. There was a door leading out to a back room and a staircase leading up the right to the next floor. Without pausing Winchester moved to the door to check the back room. The other three moved in, one watching the stairs, the other two covering Winchester. Before they could move any further they heard a scream from outside. The grenadier, a twenty two year old private from Kentucky, called Lewis moved to the front entrance to see what the commotion was.

"What can you see, Lewis?" asked Winchester.

"Looks like there's a problem back at Anders and the dead guy," he replied.

The sound of fast footsteps brought his attention back to the room that the four men were in. Winchester signalled up with his hand and the four men immediately returned to the staircase. Whatever was going on outside was of secondary importance, as a potential hostile in an elevated position on the platoon's flank could spell disaster.

Moving fast the grenadier was up first, followed by the machine gunner. As they continued moving the other two followed to take the positions the first two men had recently occupied. The room they entered was large, with only a small gap leading to a fire escape. The room took up the whole of the floor and in the centre was a table with a variety of bags and tools on it. Against the wall were about a dozen firearms of varying vintage. The four men moved around, checking for any sign of the person they'd heard. Winchester moved to the fire escape, keeping his M4 raised and ready in case of ambush. He peeked quickly outside and then ducked back inside. Nothing happened though. The others, satisfied that the room was clear of people, took up positions behind Winchester and the fire escape.

"Did you hear that?" asked Lewis.

The four men kept still, it didn't take long before they heard the same thing that Lewis had noticed. Something was being dragged upstairs.

"Follow me!" shouted Winchester as he slung his carbine down on its three point sling and moved out to the fire escape.

It was a traditional old iron staircase and led up to the roof. With just a few pulls he was at the top and peering over the edge of the flat roof to a bizarre sight. The three men below called up to find out what was going on.

"I don't get it, there are four guys up here. One is hiding in the corner and the other three are standing around him. They look weird though."

"What do you mean?" asked Lewis.

A single gunshot rang out before the conversation could go on any further. Winchester, afraid that the weapon that had just been fired may have been discharged in the street, vaulted over the low wall with his weapon at the ready. He landed on the other side onto the flat roof about thirty feet from the strangers. He moved two paces forward and then dropped to his knee, carbine at his shoulder. The other marines followed his lead and spread out, each of them training their weapons onto the group.

"Salaa day waacha ra!" Winchester shouted to them."

Though he didn't actually speak Pashtu, the marines had spent time learning the fifteen more common phrases that they would need. Winchester had told them to drop their weapons in the best Pashtu his adrenalin pumped body could manage. Drop your weapons was number four on the list! There was no response though, the three men moved closer to the man cringing on the ground.

Winchester repeated the order whilst the other three soldiers spread out, each one keeping a careful eye on the group in the corner. There was still no response. The man on the ground started muttering something and then with a single click lifted his pistol to his head and pulled the trigger, though there was no sign of the entry wound as their line of sight was blocked. The blood and gore from the back of the man's head blasted out into the air and off into the street below.

"Fuck!" shouted Lewis.

One of the men lowered himself to the body and started to bite and tear at the broken flesh of the man's head. The grenadier, a swarthy marine turned to his right and vomited onto the roof of the building. The other two men turned around to face the marines. Both of them were dressed in the usual civilian garb but they were also much paler than expected and each man had dripping blood coming from the sides of their mouths. The one to the left opened its jaw to reveal its blood covered teeth and called out in a sickening wail. They started staggering towards the marines whilst the third continued to feed on the corpse of the unfortunate man lying on the roof until a glint of light reflecting off Lewis's M4 caught its eye. It turned around, spotting the marines and cried out in the same awful tone as the others. Lifting itself up it dragged what looked like a snapped or broken leg behind it.

Winchester, not happy with the turn this room clearance had taken, took a step back and then shouted at the group.

"Wa da rey ga!" he cried, the Pashtu for stop. The group still ignored the marines and they were now only ten feet away.

Winchester raised his M4 in the air and fired a shot, hoping it would scare them off. Even this had no effect. The other three marines took a few steps back, trying to keep the distance between them but they were rapidly running out of roof. Winchester stood his ground and lowered his carbine at the chest of the closest one. He shouted for them to stop one last time and then took careful aim. The closest of the group howled and then lunged forward at the marine. He dodged to the side and smashed his carbine butt down onto the man's head, knocking him down to the ground.

He looked down to make sure man stayed down. With a groan it lifted itself up and tried to bite into his leg. With another swing he struck the man in the neck. The bones made a sickening crunch sound and he fell back with his head at an impossible angle.

The other marines were now unable to step back any further, and with their weapons lowered they shouted at the men to back off. One of the men reached out to grab at Lewis who squeezed off three rounds into the man's chest. The 5.56mm bullets easily ripped through the man's chest and hurled him to the ground. The others kept moving forwards, ignoring the plight of their comrade. Even the one on the ground started to try and lift himself back up.

"Fuck this!" shouted Winchester as he fired a single round into its head, putting it down permanently.

The rest of the men opened up, firing a conservative number of bullets into the torsos of the assailants. All but one was knocked to the ground. The man still standing managed to grab at Lewis and before any of them could stop him he tried to bite into the marine's shoulder. With a deft swing of his weapon he stuck the man in the head and then fired a dozen rounds cutting the man with a swathe of bullets from his armpit to his head. The mutilated corpse collapsed to the ground.

A crackle followed by the firm voice of Sergeant Black

whispered into Winchester's ear.

"What the fuck is going on up there?"

Back in the street Sergeant Black was trying to maintain order after the insanity of the wounded man who had tried to attack the marines. Though the man was now dead, Black was concerned at how much effort was required to actually put him down. The marines were spread out in a defensive position in the street that resembled a crescent. With the heavy weapons brought to the front they had plenty of firepower and were confident they could repel any attack if needed. The trouble was that the only movement was coming from the group heading down the street.

"We've hit problems. These guys are on something, they tried to bite and attack us. We had to defend ourselves," came the crackled radio contact from Winchester on the rooftop.

Sergeant Black was worried. He'd lost contact with Mathew's squad and the LT was proving less than useful.

"Oh, shit!" said Black.

Winchester continued, "I can see small groups coming in from the north and west. Shit, they've spotted us!"

Gunfire erupted out into the distance as streams of rifle bullets thudded into the building off to the right of Black. Insurgents were obviously now in the town, perhaps on the same mission as the marines, to find out what was going on and to reclaim the town.

Black shouted out to the marines.

"We've got insurgents approaching, keep your heads down and hold your fire!"

The marines, already in good positions, did their best to be as inconspicuous as possible whilst Black called in on the radio to the unit back at the landing zone.

"Base control, we have a situation here. Any update on Team Charlie?" he asked.

He was answered by nothing but static. He tried again but heard nothing. This wasn't good. With no reply from Mathews and his unit, and no contact from the landing zone, he now faced the very real possibility that the other two squads had been eliminated. Either way, right now he had just one squad of twelve men plus himself to defend this street and possibly the entire town.

"Fuck!" he muttered to himself. This situation had just gone from bad to shit.

The gunfire continued as heavy rounds, probably 7.62mm AKM bullets slammed into the building. Without warning the men on the rooftop returned fire with M16s, M4 carbines and the M249 SAW. The amount of fire was impressive but how much effect they had couldn't be seen from this position.

Sergeant Black signalled to the marines around him in the street to hold their fire until he gave the signal. Black hoped that if the insurgents were too busy focussing on attacking the building they might not spot the marines dug in around the crossroads. It was a possibility, and at the very least might give them the edge in the opening phase of any combat. He pulled out his binoculars and scanned the horizon for any sign of the enemy.

Torres crept up and tapped him, whispering quietly.

"Sarge, we've spotted more movement out there. See, off to the alley ahead, near the burnt out shop," he pointed.

Black examined the area. He saw a group of half a dozen men, all armed and with the traditional head scarf covering their features. At least two of them were carrying RPG launchers and the rest had AKs of various models. He scanned the area off to the right, the group of shambling civilians were still making slow progress down the street. It made no sense. He turned back to the group in the alley, one of them was missing. He double checked, spotting the man just in time to see a puff of smoke come from the RPG launcher.

"Shit!" he called, watching the trail as the rocket blasted from left to right in front of the marines. The rocket missed the building to the right and exploded against a building nearby, sending small shards of stone into the air. Machine gun fire opened up to the left and Sergeant Black was about to shout to cease fire until he spotted the group of about a dozen armed men rush around the corner, right into the marines defending the corner.

The fireteams M249 put down an impressive rate of fire. Its 5.56mm bullets tearing through the insurgents and eliminating five or six of them in the first long burst. The survivors threw themselves behind the wrecked cars and returned fire with their AKs.

Sergeant Black raised his M4 and fired a burst, hitting one of them in the head and suppressing the others. Unfortunately the surprise attack from the left had drawn the attention of the men in the alley and they now split their fire between Black's men in the street and the men on the rooftop of the building.

He raised his arm and gave the signal. Any of the marines not currently firing now added their own support to the combat. Several explosions rocked their positions as either RPGs or high explosive grenades landed short in front of the men. Scanning the area, Sergeant Black could see that their position was strong but they did have one big problem, their line of retreat was down the open street with just a few crashed cars for cover. To his left the fireteam continued to pour bullets into the Taliban soldiers who were now pinned down in the street. The other men spread out in the street near him sniping at any of the insurgents if they raised their heads. He signalled to Atkins to cover his right as the remaining men were all in the building, fighting from the rooftop.

One of the doors near the fireteam to the left ripped open to reveal a large group of probably a dozen civilians. Like the injured man they were covered in blood and gore and shambled out towards the marines. The men, already busy fighting to their front, hadn't spotted the danger and over the sound of gunfire Sergeant Black couldn't make himself heard. Tapping Torres on his shoulder the two rushed to the breach, both firing short bursts as they moved. The gunfire continued, it seemed more fighters had arrived as scores of rounds hammered into the street, forcing some of the marines to drop down low to avoid fire.

Torres and Sergeant Black managed to halt the attack of those breaking out from the room and turned their attention to forcing back the attackers in front of their hastily prepared positions in the street.

Torres shouted over to the Sergeant, "What the fuck is up with these guys?"

"I don't know, maybe there's been a chemical or biological attack in this area."

As he spoke, two of the killed Taliban fighters lifted themselves up, just twenty metres in front of their positions. They were badly injured from multiple bullet wounds and both were suffering from bizarre drooling of blood. The closest one opened his mouth, more blood oozed from it.

Black pulled out his Beretta M9A1 9mm automatic pistol. Without hesitating he squeezed off two rounds, the first to the head and the second to the centre of the body. The enemy combatant flew backwards, blood spraying from the exit wound at the back of his skull. Torres put half a clip into the other man, almost cutting his arm off. Amazingly he was still standing and started shambling towards them both. As Torres slammed in another clip a burst of M249 fire came down from the rooftop to the right. The rounds tore a line in front of the marines, both knocking down the man and also pinning the others down from the sustained fire.

Sergeant Black called up to Winchester who was still on the rooftop.

"Give me a SITREP," he called.

The answer was almost immediate, "SITREP is holy shit, Sarge!"

He continued, "We checked the bodies up here, it looks like they've been dead for several days. Somehow these fuckers are fighting us after they die."

The Sergeant looked down at the bodies near him, noticing several of them moving, even though they appeared to be dead. He thought back to what Private Bennett had said about them being like zombies. He looked up, spotting the man who was currently blazing away with his M249. He moved up, shouting into the man's ear as he kept firing.

"What did you mean when you said these things were like zombies?" he shouted.

The marine continued shooting, his fire being critical in keeping down the heads of the enemy. He turned and shouted briefly.

"They look like them and when we kill them they get up and keep fighting. It's like Night of the Living Dead out there!" he said with a grin.

Sergeant Black felt stunned. Surely not, there was no such thing. If something like this was happening, then it must be going on in other places. The images of the attacks by some kind of biological threat appeared to him.

"Oh fuck!" he called.

Looking around, their position was now being assaulted on three sides by the insurgents. Whether these things were zombies or not didn't really matter, all he needed to know was that they were hard to kill and something was very wrong.

A scream out to his left caught his attention. One of the marines had been dragged down by three or four of the things and they were biting and clawing at the man. The soldier was badly injured yet still managed to fire off a few rounds from his pistol before succumbing to his wounds. One of his comrades tried to help him only to be hit from a burst from an insurgent's Kalashnikov. The bullets punched into his body armour though amazingly one penetrated enough to cause serious injury. He fell down but still managed to keep shooting.

The group of civilians were now only twenty or so metres away and it was clear that they were suffering the same condition as the rest of the dead. First, they were dead, second, they were out for blood. Torres hurled a grenade into the mass, the blast scattering half a dozen of them and causing terrible injures on those that were close to the epicentre of the explosion. It didn't stop them though. The injured men either lifted themselves back up or crawled along the ground.

"Sarge!" A voice called.

The NCO felt himself falling down as one of the marines threw him to the floor. A group of insurgents had found a way through the alleys to sneak in on the right. The marine fired a burst from his M4 before taking the full impact of the closest insurgent's Kalashnikov in the chest. The bullets tore open his torso, killing him almost instantly. Sergeant Black, still on the floor added his own fire, managing to kill the survivors. As he turned back to the horde to the north a series of RPG rockets blasted into the marine's defensive position, the explosions blocking his visibility completely.

Up on the rooftop Winchester and his fireteam had their hands full. Though they had the best view of the action, they were also the most exposed and had already taken two minor wounds from a nearby RPG explosion. Luckily their body armour had done its job and turned what would have been a fatal injury into something that could be patched up upon their return. It was getting too dangerous to stay on the roof. He moved to the other defenders.

"This is too hot. We need to get down to the next floor

and create some loopholes. Got it?"

The others needed no encouragement. The incoming fire on the roof was now so intense the group could hardly move, let alone return fire. As the men moved down the stairs Winchester tried to contact Sergeant Black.

"Sarge, we've moving to the lower level, we're taking too much fire here."

He reached the bottom of the staircase and immediately started working on the crumbling wall to create loopholes to shoot from. Inside they could hear the noise of the battle outside.

The doorway to the fire escape ripped open to reveal an insurgent with an explosive belt around his waist. Without pausing, Lewis who was stood to the side of the door slammed his M4 carbine into the man's chest, knocking him back outside. The enemy fighter evidently hadn't expected to run into the men and accidentally triggered the charge as he fell. The blast was massive and tore open the side of the building and most of the floor the marines were occupying. Amazingly none were hurt but their position was now far less comfortable.

The marine rifleman next to Lewis laughed whilst watching the smoke and debris clear, "Stupid fucker!"

Winchester received more information from Sergeant Black.

"Get back here, we need to evac ASAP!" he shouted.

"Affirmative!" he answered and gave the signal to the

rest of the fireteam to abandon their already compromised position. As the group rushed down the stairs they came to the damaged door and the carnage outside.

The scene of the battle was incredible. When they'd left to take the building the marines were occupying a wide perimeter across the street and their situation looked secure. Now the street was full of smoke and debris whilst tracer and bullets whistled by from almost every direction. Worse though was that it seemed a large number of the dead inhabitants were rising from the ground and moving in to encircle the marines' defensive position. Of the original three fireteams there were now only seven marines plus Sergeant Black. In the battle five had been killed and it looked like most of the rest had sustained injuries, though so far none of them seemed fatal. As they moved out into the street they added their own fire to that of the surviving marines. Sergeant Black was flanked by Fernanda and Torres who were pinned down behind a burnt out wreck of a Toyota Corolla.

Winchester moved up to the Sergeant, shouting over the gunfire.

"We need to retreat, Sarge," he screamed.

Sergeant Black knocked down three of the walking corpses with an accurate series of bursts from his M4 and then slammed in another magazine.

"No shit, son. Is your radio still working? Last I heard was that we have evac coming in to the LZ in fifteen minutes."

"I'm just hitting static," he shouted over the din of the firefight.

From all four directions the undead locals were now shambling towards them. The real problem though was the number of insurgents who were using them as cover to get closer to attack the marines. Sergeant Black needed no encouragement to leave the scene.

"Come on marines, follow me!" he shouted as he moved off to the left and into the alleyway.

The other seven followed in quick succession with Winchester covering the rear. As they rounded the first corner they ran into three of the walking corpses. Without stopping Black smashed the first one down with the butt of his M4 and then fired three short bursts into each of them. In literally three seconds they were past the bodies and moving deeper into the back streets. An RPG whistled by, missing the unit and hitting one of the houses a short distance away. The shock of the attacker being so close forced the marines close to the walls of the buildings but they kept on moving, firing at any targets as they emerged.

They now turned left onto a long alleyway that ran parallel to the main street. From what Black remembered this route took them almost directly back to the LZ. He signalled to the marines to keep moving whilst he spoke to Torres.

"You got any power left in your phone?" he asked, expecting to hear him bitch and whine about the battery life issues once more.

Torres flipped the phone out of a pouch and held it in the shade of the wall to view the screen.

"Yeah, Sarge, I've got one bar of power and a signal."

"Fuck yeah!" answered Sergeant Black.

"Call HQ, tell them they'll be coming in hot. We need extraction from the LZ in eight minutes, no later. Got it?" he continued.

Torres nodded and hit the emergency contact the marines were all given in case of radio issues. At least one good thing had come from watching Heartbreak Ridge all those years ago!

The rest of the unit kept moving, they couldn't afford to stop as the number of the walking corpses in the town seemed to be increasing, with the majority right behind the marines. More of the creatures appeared ahead, blocking the alley with their numbers. Just as the marines were about to change direction a three man group of insurgents appeared just feet from the walking dead. With a scream, the first was dragged down, teeth and hands tearing at his body. The other two tried to run but fire from the marines stopped them in their tracks.

The insurgent was still screaming yet the marines did nothing. Fernanda, in contrast to the others, aimed her rifle down the street and pulled the trigger but the barrel was knocked up by Winchester, the bullets blasted off harmlessly into the air.

"What the fuck!" she shouted.

Sergeant Black towered in front of them, "Fuck em! It's time for payback, come on!"

He moved off down a narrow alley to the right and then took a hard left, still moving in roughly the same direction as before so they could reach the landing zone. As the insurgent started to disappear from view, Winchester gave him one last glance. The man was reaching down for something. Before the marine could respond the enemy soldier vanished in a flash of light and smoke, he'd obviously decided to use his suicide belt.

"At last, a fucking use for the bastards!" he muttered to himself.

He rejoined the survivors as they continued their retreat to the landing zone. Tracer fire hit down the alley, as more insurgents moved in to surround the beleaguered marines. Two of the riflemen were cut down before the rest could take cover. As they returned fire the telltale smoke trails of two RPG rockets blasted towards them.

"Come on!" shouted Sergeant Black as he lifted himself up and zigzagged down the narrow alley and into the open space beyond.

The marines followed, each firing short bursts behind them at the distant targets. As Sergeant Black left the outskirts of the town he slid down behind the first rocks he found. Lifting his weapon he fired repeatedly into the pursuing enemy, now unclear whether they were walking corpses or the Taliban. Either way they needed to die. The rest of the marines tumbled out of the dust and debris filled alley, first Torres, then Fernanda and then a massive blast. The entire alley disappeared in flashes of fire and smoke as multiple RPG rockets peppered the area. More gunfire hit the scene and it looked like nobody else could possibly survive.

Black, Torres and Fernanda all took cover in the rocks, taking pot shots at any targets as they emerged from the many alleys and lanes in the town. They were down to their rifles and M4s, no machineguns now left in their hands.

Sergeant Black lifted himself up carefully, still watching for survivors. The sound of an aircraft, possibly a helicopter could just be heard coming from the south. He turned to see how far away it was, by his estimate they had probably two minutes till it reached them. The LZ was literally thirty seconds jog from their position in the rocks though there was no sign of the marines or the LT.

Another explosion blasted the edge of the town. The three kept low, avoiding the debris and more frequent rifle fire. As the smoke and debris cleared an injured, but still standing, Winchester staggered out.

"Holy shit!" shouted Torres as he ran down to help the man.

Sergeant Black gave Fernanda a grim look.

"We need to get to the LZ, you give Torres a hand, I'll look for the LT," he ordered.

Black moved up to the ridge and the LZ whilst the other two marines moved down to help Winchester.

Black scrambled up the ridge, making it to the top in just seconds. He was astonished to find the position deserted. There were no weapons, equipment or marines. He scanned the area quickly but still no sign. As he turned to check on the progress of Winchester he spotted movement in the small blockhouse. He looked carefully, spotting the shape of a man inside. Without pausing he ran to the building and kicked open the door. Inside was the cowering figure of Lieutenant Wade. The Sergeant leaned towards him and grabbed the man, yanking him up and then dragged him out of the room.

"Sir, where is 1st Squad?" he shouted.

Lieutenant Wade muttered something incomprehensible. Sergeant Black, now lacking patience simply ignored the muttering and shouted at him.

"Where the fuck are they, Sir? Where are my men?"

The aircraft was now just a few hundred metres away. It was another of the V-22 Osprey tiltrotor aircraft. It circled the position and gunfire poured from the rear ramp position where a marine manned a machinegun.

The other three survivors were now up with Sergeant Black, watching both the Osprey and the distant town for hostiles.

"Sarge!" shouted Torres, pointing to the main street.

He turned to see a dull red Toyota Hilux pickup tearing down the road. On the bed of the truck were half a dozen insurgents, all heavily armed. The ground around the marines now threw up tonnes of debris as the Osprey came in low to land, its rear facing the marines and the gunner still shooting.

"Get in!" shouted Black as he led the group to the ramp.

In just seconds the marines were aboard and the aircraft was already climbing steadily away from the town. The gunner fired a few more shots then stopped as they moved out of range.

Lieutenant Wade sat alongside Black in the aircraft and had already started to regain some of his composure, now that the unit was safe and leaving the area. He looked around the aircraft and was about to speak when he uncontrollably spasmed. With a heavy cough a mouthful of congealed blood dripped out of his mouth onto the floor of the craft. Winchester and Torres moved back inside the Osprey whilst Sergeant Black lifted himself up to face the officer.

"You been bitten, Sir?" he asked suspiciously.

The officer looked at his left arm, cradling a wounded arm.

"It's your fault you fucks. You abandoned me!" he cried.

Torres made a move towards him to punch the man, only to be stopped by Fernanda.

"He's not worth it, man. Leave it for his court martial!"

Wade seemed disinterested by the unfolding drama. He looked around at them all.

"Court martial? Fuck you all, fuck you all, you disobeyed my orders!" he whined.

Sergeant Black pointed out through the open cargo ramp at something.

"Holy shit, did you see that?" he asked.

Wade turned around for a better view, squinting at the bright light from the unrelenting Afghan sun. Black gave a brief look at the filthy and exhausted marines, spotting the nod from Fernanda and with one swift motion slammed his boot into Wade's lower back, knocking him out of the cabin and down the rear ramp. Wade turned around trying to grab at something, anything that would stop him falling. It was too late though and with one last stumble he fell from the rear of the Osprey, tumbling to the arid Afghan terrain below.

Fernanda watched him fall, shouting as she watched him drop, "Die you spineless fuck!"

It took only a few moments for Wade's body to hit the ground, the impact on the hard ground instantly breaking his back. Blood spurted from his mouth and he choked on the blood in his lungs. He had just seconds to live and yet he struggled to look up at the bright sky. The mortally wounded officer spotted something approaching, it was the red Toyota.

As it stopped nearby a number of insurgents approached leaning down and pulling at him and his equipment. With a cough and one last splutter he died.

As the Taliban soldiers stripped the officer of his webbing and equipment the oldest noticed movement in the body. He leaned in closely, pushing the head back with his Kalashnikov. The man's face was pale and blood was dripping from his mouth. Before he realised what was happening the American lurched forwards and sank his teeth into the militant's throat.

CHAPTER EIGHT

Bristol, England

Driving through the suburbs of the city was a truly depressing sight. All around them were bodies, both dead and walking. Cars were scattered about the streets, the odd building was on fire, rubbish was scattered everywhere. The creatures were less of a problem now that they were in a car, but they couldn't drive forever. Gary was driving as quickly as he could, considering the circumstances. Too slow and any chance of saving his family would be at risk, too fast and the danger of a collision or damage to the underside of the car increased.

"Get a fucking shift on, mate!" shouted Matt.

"Don't push me, I'm going as fast as is sensible," said Gary.

"Fuck sensible, put your foot down!" shouted Matt.

"Quit whining like a little girl and start taking this seriously!" shouted Gary.

As they approached a four way junction two vehicles raced past in front of them, with no caution for any other potential survivors. They were probably some of the few survivors in the area, but it was now every man for himself. As they passed the junction they could see a large scattering of creatures in the direction from where the vehicles had come from.

The area was eerily silent as they drove down dirty and bloodied streets, evading the creatures they encountered. It was a busy city that they were used to working in, now there was just the sound of the odd car that people were using to escape the devastation. They could hear the odd scream from shops and houses that they drove past, but it was too late for those people.

"We're just a few streets away now, so be ready," said Gary.

"For what?" asked Matt.

"Honestly I don't know, just be alert," said Gary.

Turning the bend they found a several car pileup. A minibus was overturned and some other cars had smashed into it, there was no way through. Gary brought their car to a standstill, whilst thinking of the best response.

"Go around?" asked Matt.

"No, it's only a short walk from here, and the car has too little fuel to get us far after we get to the house anyway," said Gary.

"Fucking wonderful," said Matt.

"Yeh, well come up with a better solution and we'll do it," said Gary.

"Alright, alright, let's get on with it," said Matt.

Gary cut the engine and the two men got out with their weapons. It was quite clear that any idiot could outrun these zombies, but the idea of being stuck on foot in a city full of them was a frightful thought.

"Stick close and follow me," said Gary.

The two men walked up to the crashed vehicles and looked into the wrecked Mondeo that was closest to them. The driver was still sitting in his seat, keeled over the steering wheel. Matt looked in to see if the man was still alive, a natural instinct from their day job. His elbow guard knocked the pillar of the door and the driver suddenly twisted and looked up at Matt. The copper quickly leapt back in shock as he realised that it was a zombie. Fortunately, the creature was firmly trapped within the damaged vehicle, held in place by the steering column crushing its torso into the seat. It pulled in every direction to try and get free, desperate to reach the men.

"Jesus that was close," said Matt.

"No shit, next time don't get near to anything resembling a person without prodding them first," said Gary.

"Fair play," said Matt.

The two men climbed onto the bonnet of the car and

used it as a stepping stone to get over the wreckage before them. Gary hoisted himself onto the overturned minibus to get a better look at their surroundings. He stood up on the chassis of the vehicle. Looking around he could see no signs of life, only a few staggering creatures.

"Mate, what are the chances your wife and kid are alive?" asked Matt.

"Don't talk that way, we'll know soon enough," said Gary.

"And what if they're zombies?" asked Matt.

"We'll cross that bridge when we come to it," said Gary.

"You reckon you can handle it?" asked Matt.

"Fuck you, have some faith," said Gary.

The men's presence up high and visible was already attracting attention from nearby shamblers, compounded by the racket they'd made clambering onto the wreckage.

"Let's move on," said Gary.

They jumped down from the vehicle and headed on down the street, it wasn't far now to Gary's home. They were walking at a steady pace, approaching a bend with two creatures on it. Gary punched the first one in the face whilst holding his baton and connecting with the carbon fibre knuckles of his riot gloves. The zombie crashed to the ground, still alive, but at least out of the way.

Matt approached his as if to strike to the head, but re-directed at the last minute, hitting the creature's knee cap dead on, the joint buckled and sent the creature onto its other knee. Whilst still in motion he swung the baton around and cracked his opponent on the back of the head, sending it face first and dead to the ground. They kept going along the street.

It was quite clear that they needed some better weapons. The batons were designed as semi-lethal weapons, but needed a lot of strength, effort and accuracy to kill a zombie. Not only that, but multiple blows were often needed, wasting valuable time.

"Mate, do you really think that your family could have survived this?" asked Matt.

"Don't talk like that," said Gary.

"I'm serious, what happens if we get there and find only zombies?" asked Matt.

"Then we'll deal with it, just shut up!" said Gary.

"Great plan," said Matt.

"Fuck you, just keep doing your part," said Gary.

"So I'm just along to kill things?" asked Matt.

"For now, yes," said Gary.

"So you got any weapons at home?" asked Matt.

"Oh yeh, I've a sawn off under the bed and a handgun in my sock drawer. What do you think?" said Gary.

"Alright, seriously though, what have you got?" asked Matt.

"A machete and a katana, that's it," said Gary.

"Well that's better than nothing."

The two men reached the corner of the street where

they could see Gary's home. Their hearts sunk as they could see a number of creatures going in through the smashed front door. There were likely to be more already inside the house. Gary's attention was drawn to movement in the front window on the upper floor.

"Chris!" shouted Gary.

"What?" asked Matt.

"It's my son!" said Gary.

Gary ran towards his house.

"Hang on mate, this is a shit plan," said Matt.

"Just follow me!" shouted Gary.

It was indeed a terrible strategy, running into a house full of enemies, but Gary was thinking single-mindedly and Matt could not reason with him. Matt knew all too well now that splitting up could be the end of both of them, so despite the awful plan of attack, he could only follow and do his best.

They reached the front door. Gary hit the first creature from behind with his shield, smashing it into the door frame. He smashed his truncheon multiple times into the back of the zombie's skull until the creature slid down the doorway, dead. Gary was no longer acting with the cool, calculated head he normally would, but as if in a frenzy. Going through the doorway he punched the face of an incoming creature, kicked it in the stomach, kneed it in the head and finally hit it to the floor with his shield. Before the creature could recover he smashed his truncheon onto the back of its skull with full force, trapping it between the weapon and the floor. The impact was hard, sending pain through his arm and especially his elbow.

It was already clear to them, that whilst they were quite capable of winning in combat against these zombies, they would quickly tire. Gary stepped over the body of the latest zombie and into the hallway of his house. It was narrow, only wide enough for one man, but it was already clogged by several creatures. The house was infested, and they were here for a reason. It was hopeful that at least one of Gary's family was still alive, as the zombies showed such drive to get into the place.

Gary continually drove his way through the creatures before him. Several turned to face this new threat, or potential for blood. He kept them at bay with his shield, whilst continually striking until they were down on the floor. Matt struck the bodies as he reached them, just to be certain. Both men had witnessed the risk of not ensuring these beasts were fully dead.

The living room and hallway were now awash with bodies and blood. Gary finally reached the bottom of the stairs. Looking up he could see a zombie beating on the door where he'd seen his son. The creature turned as it was alerted by the policeman's presence.

Gary finally realised what he now faced, the bloodthirsty creature before him was his wife. Blood dripped from her jaw, her clothes were torn and dirty, her flesh ripped and cut. Gary couldn't move or speak, he was in too much shock.

"What is it, mate?" asked Matt.

"That's Sandra," said Gary.

"Your wife?" asked Matt.

Gary nodded slowly as the creature began to stagger down the steps towards him. He was still unable to move, his weapons hanging at his sides.

"Mate, you're going to have to do something," said Matt.

"Like what?" asked Gary.

"Kill the bitch," said Matt.

"That's my wife!" shouted Gary.

"Not anymore, she's a zombie who's stopping you getting to your son!" shouted Matt.

His former wife was now halfway down the stairs but Gary had still made no move at all, completely stunned and shocked by the situation. He'd gone from utter frenzy to depressive nothingness.

"Then get out the way and let me do it," said Matt.

"No, this is my job," said Gary.

"Good, you're doing her a favour, she would never want to be this way," said Matt.

"That doesn't make it any easier," said Gary.

"It should do, you'll be doing the kindest thing, now man the fuck up and do what you know you have to do!" shouted Matt.

Sandra was just two steps from the bottom of the stairs where Gary stood as he lifted his baton. He could not bring himself to kill his wife, even if she was now a zombie. She reached him and grabbed at his shoulders. The creature was desperately trying to pull him closer in order to bite him, but he was keeping her at a distance with his shield pushed into her chest.

"Do it!" shouted Matt.

"No!" shouted Gary.

Matt stepped in closer and smashed his truncheon down onto the creature's head, knocking her flat onto the stairs. He grabbed Gary's chest armour and heaved him out of the way before finally smashing the baton down on the zombie's head to finish her off. Gary, having regained his footing, ran at Matt, shoving him against the wall.

"What the hell are you doing?" shouted Gary.

"It had to be done and you know it," said Matt.

"That was my wife!" shouted Gary.

"Not anymore!" replied Matt.

Gary released his hold on his friend and looked down at the bloody lifeless mess of his wife sprawled at the bottom of the stairs in their home. Gary had longed for action and adventure in his life, to break away from the boredom, but this was not at all what he'd anticipated.

"I'm sorry, mate. I didn't want it either," said Matt.

Gary collapsed down on his sofa, traumatised by the day. He had little will left in him to even stand.

"What about your son?" asked Matt.

Gary suddenly sprung to life. The brutal killing of his zombified wife had made him completely forget about Chris. He leapt from the sofa and ran upstairs, not at all bothered now by having to step over the corpse of his wife. He reached the top of the stairs and the door to the room he'd seen his son. It was the bathroom, the only one with a lock, and it was locked. He hammered on the door.

"Chris! Chris?" shouted Gary.

There was no response. Matt looked up from the bottom of the stairs, the silence was unbearable. He knocked on the door again.

"Chris, are you ok?"

"Daddy?" asked Chris.

Gary's heart raced at the response he finally got, to hear anyone talking anymore was a major relief.

"Yes, it's me. Open the door, son," said Gary.

"But, but, how do I know you're not one of the monsters?" asked Chris.

"You'll have to trust me Chris, I'm here to rescue you," said Gary.

"But what if you become like Mummy?" asked Chris.

"It's ok, Chris. I'm ok, and so is my partner Matt, but we have to get away from here, to a safe place," said Gary.

"In here is safe, the monsters can't get in," said Chris.

"But you can't stay in there forever, son. You haven't got any food or water," said Gary.

"Where's Mummy?" asked Chris.

"She's gone now, she can't hurt you," said Gary.

There was a long silence as Chris thought about what to do. The bathroom was the only place of safety he'd known. The fact that one parent had turned on him frightened him a lot. Finally he crept up to the door and opened it. Gary snatched him into his arms.

"Chris, are you ok?" asked Gary.

"Yes, but Mummy bit me," said Chris.

Gary's heart sank as the reality of the situation dawned on him. He pulled Chris back into his view to see the cut flesh on his son's arm, blood seeped from the wound. This was likely the man's only family left in the world, and he already knew that would now only last a matter of hours at best. Tears began to stream from his eyes, but he pulled Chris into his arms to conceal his distraught state. He no longer knew what to do, his wife now dead, his son soon to be. Matt walked into the room and could see the pale sad face of his friend.

"What's up?" asked Matt.

"Sandra bit him," said Gary.

Matt gasped in disbelief. After all the effort and trauma they'd gone through to save Gary's family, this is what it had come to. He now wished, they both did, that they'd not gone to his house at all. Sadly, the chance of leaving his family behind was not one that Gary could ever have lived with.

"What do you want to do?" asked Matt.

"I have no idea," said Gary.

Gary thought long and hard about all of the possibilities. He was trying with all his energy to disassociate himself with his son, knowing full well what had to be done.

"Do you want me to do it?" asked Matt.

"No, wait downstairs," said Gary.

"Sure?" asked Matt.

"Yeh, go," said Gary.

Matt went downstairs and sat down on the leather sofa in the living room. He relaxed back in comfort, ignoring the bodies of their victims lying around him. A few moments later Gary walked back down the stairs, looking terrible.

"Have you done it?" asked Matt.

"No," said Gary.

"You know it has to be done!" shouted Matt.

"No I don't! What is one more zombie in the world? He won't know any different and we won't be around to see otherwise," said Gary.

Matt thought about what his friend had said and understood. If leaving him to become a zombie maintained some sanity for his friend, so be it.

"So what have you done with him?" asked Matt.

"I told him to stay there where he felt safe, and to lock the door, as we were going to help some other people," said Gary.

"And he accepted that?" asked Matt.

"Yes, it's the only place in the world where he feels comfortable and safe, it's the best way," said Gary.

Matt said nothing more, as dwelling on the matter would only make things harder for Gary. They both now needed to maintain a solid frame of mind and cool headedness.

"So what do we do now?" asked Matt.

"We clearly can't stay here, there are zombies everywhere. We either find somewhere that's fortified, or escape to the countryside," said Gary.

"What would we do in the country?" asked Matt.

"Well there are less people there, so less zombies," said Gary.

"But what do we know about the countryside, we aren't fucking farm boys," said Matt.

"Then we find somewhere secure with food and drink," said Gary.

"Sounds like a plan, like where?" asked Matt.

"Only place I can think of is The Mall, very secure and full of supplies," replied Gary.

"Alright, you got a car?" asked Matt.

"I've got a bike, and that'll be easier to get around with anyway, the roads are all going to be packed," said Gary.

Gary grabbed the katana from the mantelpiece and handed it to Matt.

"Fucking cool," said Matt.

Gary took a machete from a cupboard by the TV and

they were now ready to go. They knew they would have to leave their shields behind, as they couldn't carry them on the bike. Despite this, the thought of getting to safety was enough to subdue their concerns. They tucked the new weapons into the strapping of their riot armour and set out from the front door. Looking at the road before them there were zombies everywhere, stumbling towards them.

"Get to the bike, run!" shouted Gary.

They ran quickly forwards to the road where Gary's bike was parked. Six creatures stood between them and the motorcycle, whilst countless others bore down on them from beyond the vehicle. Matt drew his katana and ran for the first creature. He hacked into the collar of his first target with a strong diagonal cut, it drove into its spine and dropped the creature to the pavement.

Gary drew his machete into his right hand and baton in the left, he charged at the first zombie, all too aware of the need for speed. He smashed the creature's face with the baton, knocking it downwards and exposing the neck. He swung the machete down with all his force to the back of the neck and the head was cleaved off, spurting blood out across the street. He ran to his next target and cut across the face with his machete, carving it open and the creature spun to the ground.

Matt reached his next opponent and cut vertically into the centre of the skull, the acutely sharp and curved blade driving deep into the brain. He kicked the beast back, pulling the sword from its head as he did so. Matt finally swung horizontally with the katana at his third opponent. His inexperience with the weapon led to poor accuracy and the blade imbedded in the shoulder, almost taking the arm off. He slid the blade from the wound and cut again, this time cutting the head down to the shoulders.

Gary cut down onto the head of his third opponent, hacking twice more until the beast collapsed into a bloody pile before him.

The men were clearly aware of the insurmountable odds, they couldn't fight on through the mass of monsters. Gary leapt onto his bike and twisted the ignition on. Matt jumped on the bike as the engine of the powerful Ducati roared to life.

Gary pushed back the kick stand and locked the bike into gear. As he put the power down, a zombie grabbed Matt from behind and wrenched him off the bike. Gary had already gone thirty feet by the time he'd realised his friend was missing, slamming the breaks on and spinning the bike around. Matt was back on his feet with his sword drawn, but his helmet was off and blood seeped from his collar.

"Go!" shouted Matt.

Gary knew all too well that anyone who was bitten was a lost cause, a hard fact to accept. Despite this, he did what was best, spinning the back tyre as he raced off. Leaving his friend behind was a dreadful feeling, but he was partially relieved that his partner was going down fighting, and not the subject of some euthanisation.

Gary continued on his journey alone, with nothing more than his riot armour and two hand weapons. He got a mile towards The Mall when he suddenly noticed an oil slick pouring from an overturned lorry. It was too late. He slammed the brakes on but slid into the slippery liquid. The bike quickly turned onto its side, sending him sliding down the road. Finally he slammed into the side of a parked car.

Despite the shock of the crash, he was on his feet within seconds. Gary felt like crap, but staying on the ground was the instant way to death and destruction. He was now covered in oil down his back and one side. He ached in a number of places, bruised and battered, though his body armour had done him proud. He wondered if it was even worth going on, his bike was his last friend in the world, and that was now destroyed, having tumbled into another vehicle and buckled. His friends and family were gone, his city in ruins, what was worth living for?

Despite all the setbacks and negative feelings, his natural instinct to live kept him moving. Getting to The Mall was all that mattered now. He could only hope that some other intelligent souls had the same idea. More than anything in life now, Gary needed allies. No man could survive alone in this world, he would be quickly overcome or lose all will to live in this frightful apocalypse. For an hour he marched on despite his aching joints. He fought only when he had no choice, when the zombies could not be avoided.

Eventually, now thoroughly exhausted, he was in sight of The Mall. The large car park was almost empty, an odd picture in the day time. He could only imagine that the shoppers fled in panic after witnessing the day's events on the news. This was fortunate for him, as the last thing he needed was his refuge full of the creatures.

He reached the main front doors of The Mall, they were locked. The re-enforced glass was near unbreakable, and even if you could break it, that would be rather unproductive in the long run. Gary heard the noise of people, a warming feeling that he'd already become unfamiliar with. He walked down the outer wall of the building until he could see some people on the roof. Looking around, a few creatures were already approaching, but they were few and far between. He reached the position below the people on the roof.

"How can I get in?" he shouted to them.

"Have you been bitten?" a man replied.

"Come on how do I get in?" shouted Gary.

"Please, just answer the question!" the man shouted back.

"No, I haven't been fucking bitten, now let me in!"

"How can we be certain?" asked the man.

Gary held up his hands and turned around to show

himself to them.

"Are you happy now?" asked Gary.

The man turned to the others on the roof top. The group was clearly in discussion as to whether they helped him to get in or not, though Gary couldn't hear them.

"Come on, I haven't got all day!" shouted Gary.

Finally, a line of sheets tied together was thrown down from the roof.

"You expect me to climb up?" asked Gary.

"Sorry, but we've closed off all the doors, this is the best way," said the man.

Gary took hold of the makeshift rope, he tugged on it to test its strength. He began to climb, it was tough work. He wasn't near enough as fit as he wished, with the day's work and his armour not helping in the slightest. Despite this, the wall allowed his legs to do some of the work, and his raw survival instincts provided him with all the determination he needed to get him up there.

After what seemed like an age, he reached the top of the wall he'd climbed, perhaps forty feet. Gary's body was bruised and battered, his clothes filthy and torn, his joints aching. The people helped pull him over the lip onto the flat roof. He stood up, but not upright, he was arched over panting from physical exhaustion.

"Hi, I'm Gary," he said.

"You're a copper?" asked the man.

"Yes," said Gary.

"Where are the rest of you?" he asked.

"Dead or dying," said Gary.

The man looked around at the two others, a man and a woman. They were clearly shocked at his response. The group knew the situation was bad, but it was clearly far worse than they had anticipated.

"I'm Patrick, this is Greg and Jessica," said the man.

Gary pulled off his glove and reached out to shake hands with his new friends.

The situation was bleak, but at least he wouldn't face it alone.

CHAPTER NINE

Queensland, Australia

It was the second day that Bruce and his band had hit the road with no particular destination or purpose. They had spent the night in a gas station that was miles from any town, but by morning the creatures were already on the horizon.

"So what's the plan now?" asked Dylan.

"I guess we keep moving, stay safe, wait for the army to do something," said Bruce.

"You reckon the diggers will sort this out?" asked Dylan.

"Who knows, but what else can we do?" said Bruce.

"So we just keep driving?" asked Dylan.

"At least we stay alive," said Bruce.

"What the hell is that?" asked Dylan

The two men squinted to make out what they could see up ahead. There was a large vehicle silhouetted against a rock formation up ahead, just fifty yards off the road. As they closed in on its position, Bruce wearily drew up. It was a Bushmaster, an armoured military truck. He stopped fifty feet short of it, not knowing what to expect. He got out and looked across at the vehicle, there was no sign of life nearby.

"Grab your weapons, let's check this out," said Bruce.

"Why?" said Connor.

"He's right, I don't like the look of this at all," said Dylan.

"Right now we need guns more than anything else in this world. That is an army truck which clearly has at least something of interest," said Bruce.

He pointed out at the pintle mounted machine gun on the roof of the wagon. It was a tempting idea.

"If that's still up there, where are the men?" asked Christian.

It was a fair point. The obvious conclusion was that they'd been killed, but then this was a remote area with no sign of enemy.

"Stop thinking and start walking," said Bruce.

The group grabbed their prospective weapons and headed over to the Bushmaster. The re-enactors had put all the armour they had with them on in the morning. That protection had saved Bruce's life once already, he'd be damned if he was going to take it off, discomfort was a small price to pay for his life.

Despite the men having their armour, none had helmets, due to the quick exit they were forced to make. All of them were irritable, the smell of sweat dripping through there gambesons. They approached the big truck from behind, where their car was parked. Staying at a good distance, Bruce moved around the vehicle to survey the situation. It became quickly clear that the heavy beast was not parked there but had crashed. It had ploughed directly into the boulders, clearly veering from the road. The Protected Mobility Vehicle, was fully enclosed.

"Shame its trashed, we could have used a rig like this," said Connor.

"This looks dodgy mate, let's get out of here while we have our skin," said Dylan.

"Not till we have some tasty hardware," said Bruce.

Bruce moved to the rear door of the vehicle and pulled the handle down, heaving the heavy door open. The body of a soldier tumbled out onto him, knocking him to the ground. He fumbled anxiously to throw the body aside and get to his feet.

"Fuck me dead!" said Bruce.

The group looked down at the body. A bullet hole was the most obvious feature, puncturing its skull almost directly between the eyes. This one was permanently dead. Bruce looked inside through the door. There were eight soldiers visible, all were motionless. He moved to the door and pushed his poleaxe in to poke a few, just to be safe.

A number of the men had gunshot wounds. Clearly there had been a firefight in this confined space, two of the dead still held handguns in their lifeless hands.

"There's some nice kit in here, we need to get the bodies out so we can get access to it all," said Bruce.

"That's pretty rough, mate," said Dylan.

"Get used to it, all that matters now is our survival, and if that means shooting a friend in the head to save the rest, you do it!" said Bruce.

He threw down his poleaxe and grabbed the closest dead soldier by the yoke of his webbing and tugged him out onto the sand. His friends watched in amazement as he dragged the body clear of the doorway so that he could pillage anything useful.

"Dylan, keep guard and watch, Connor, Christian, start pulling those bodies out!" said Bruce.

Connor and Christian simply looked at each other, feeling sick at the very thought. Bruce was busy ripping off anything useful from the body, primarily the ammunition.

"Go on, get to it!" said Bruce.

The two men crept up to the truck, sickened by the sight before them. The men had pulled four bodies out when Christian reached for the fifth. As he took hold of the body's clothing, its eyes opened and hands grabbed his forearm. Before Christian could get free, the soldier bit down on to his arm. The zombie's jaws drove deeply into his gambeson, but the thickly quilted garment was too deep to be penetrated.

Amassing all his strength, Christian pulled the zombie from its seat, its jaw still firmly rooted in his sleeve. He wrenched the creature hard so that its head pounded against the opposite wall of the truck. The impact caused it to release and drop to the floor. Not waiting a moment for it to recover, he stamped on the creature's head until it fractured open, spilling blood out across the floor.

"Bit jumpy there, mate," said Bruce sarcastically.

"Fuck you!" said Christian.

Connor was busy stripping the dead of all their equipment when Christian finally got to the far end of the cabin, where he found something rather appealing.

"Hey, Bruce!" said Christian.

Bruce looked around to see Christian at the hatch of the truck wielding an F89 machinegun. This was a lightweight sustained fire weapon with a belt driven large box magazine. It was still quite a weight, but a handy package compared to the weighty GPMG that was mounted up top on the vehicle.

"Fucking Dinky-di," said Bruce.

"It's not my bowl of rice, want it?" asked Christian.

"Fuck, yeh," said Bruce.

He took the gun, known as a Minimi from his friend. He looked thoroughly impressed with his new toy. This might have been a disgusting task to have had to do, but all the men were now feeling a whole lot happier about themselves.

"Load all the guns and any ammo you can find into the UTE, then we'll be off," said Bruce.

It was a good haul. Within five minutes they'd gained a Minimi, seven F88 AuSteyrs, two Browning HI-Powers and a good stash of ammunition. The Steyr was always a funny looking weapon, with the magazine behind the trigger. It looked like something from a sci-fi movie. The handguns could well come in useful.

"Connor, get up on top and grab that machinegun," said Bruce.

"What are we going to do with that?" asked Connor.

"You let me worry about that, get your arse up there!" said Bruce.

Within a few minutes the man had lugged the big lump of metal down from the truck. It was an FN MAG, more powerful than anything else they had, and much heavier.

"I am not lugging this piece of shit around!" said Connor.

"Stop bitching you sissy, chuck it in the car," said Bruce.

"You know what I would love?" said Dylan.

"A coldie?" said Bruce.

"Exactly, mate," said Dylan.

"Agreed, let's get back on the road, perhaps we can do something about that," said Bruce.

"Shotgun," said Connor.

"Fuck off," said Dylan.

Dylan jumped into the passenger seat before Connor could snap the privilege and luxury away from him. A few moments later the Holden was kicking up sand and dirt and storming down the road. You would think at a time like this that any man would do his best to conserve fuel, but not Bruce. Any spark of excitement was worth it now.

The group had gathered a decent amount of food and drink from the gas station the night before. With a full tank of gas, a couple of full jerry cans and plenty of hardware, they were as best equipped as anyone could be at this time. Sadly they lacked one key feature, somewhere safe. Every building out of the cities was no more secure than a car. They could do nothing but drive on.

"So we heading for the smoke or outback?" asked Dylan.

"I guess we'll just keep going and see what happens," said Bruce.

"Great plan," said Dylan.

"Got anything better?" said Bruce.

"Nope," said Dylan.

"Exactly," said Bruce.

Out ahead on the open plain they could see a dust cloud, the familiar sight associated with a car tumbling through the dusty roads. A few moments later it came into view, a sedan. Bruce drew the car to a halt, clearly hoping for some kind of discussion. The men waited impatiently, glad to see another sign of life.

The car didn't slow down, but merely stormed past them, kicking up sand and stones in to their faces. Bruce looked at his poor car, the purple shine of the paintwork now dulled by a couple of days of grime. They looked into the car as it raced past at maybe eighty miles an hour. There was just one man, the driver. The group looked back at the car racing away from them.

"What is he doing?" asked Connor.

"Looks like a man on a mission," said Dylan.

The speeding car's brakes were slammed on. A new cloud of dust was kicked up as the harsh sound of brakes rung out. The car had spun around and was now heading back towards them, again at speed. The sedan reached the group and its brakes were again slammed on, screeching the car to a halt next to them. The man wound down his window to look at the men, he looked a little surprised. This was to be expected, it is not every day that you see people in medieval plate armour carrying machineguns.

"Where you heading?" asked Bruce.

"To find my wife," said the man.

"Why?" said Bruce.

"Because she's my wife," the man replied.

"What's the point? She'll be dead, dying or undead, none of which is helpful," said Bruce.

"She might have survived," said the man.

"People are dying all around, and you think one woman might have managed to make it through. Wake up!" said Bruce.

"What my friend is trying to say is, don't throw your life away. We've just come from that way. It's nothing but death and destruction," said Dylan.

"Come with us, we have a chance," said Bruce.

"No, I have to find my wife, she's all I have left!" the man said.

"No, all you have left is your car and your skin, two of the most valuable assets in the world today," said Bruce.

"Sorry, but I have to do this," said the man.

Dylan took one of the rifles from the car and handed it through the window to the man.

"What are you doing?" asked Bruce.

"We've got more than we need, we can't let him drive to his death without at least some assistance," said Dylan.

"Oh what a fucking good Samaritan you are!" said Bruce.

The man took the rifle, not really knowing how to even hold it, he placed it into the foot well of the passenger side. The man was edgy, scared, it was obvious he would not last long with the odds against him, but who were they do stop him? Safety in numbers was of course preferable at this time, but only if every one of those numbers was a capable ally.

"Thank you, and good luck," the driver said.

"And to you," said Dylan.

The man rolled up his window and spun the car around, tearing off into the distance.

"Right, let's move the fuck on before you give away the rest of our arsenal to useless fuckwits," said Bruce.

He jumped into the Holden and they were back on their way. All wondered what had become of everyone else they knew in their lives. All of these men full well accepted that any friends and family were either dead, or had made their own way to safety. Going in search of anything except food, shelter, gas or weapons was now futile.

A couple of hours later they came to the sign to a small town, population of around three hundred.

"This could be a handy place to find a few coldies," said Bruce.

Dylan snorted as he woke to the sound of a chilled beer being mentioned. The men had fallen into a broken sleep, tired physically and emotionally. The focus of driving was all that had kept Bruce awake.

"You should let me drive soon," said Dylan.

"You're not touching this baby," said Bruce.

"And what happens if we get into a fight and you are too exhausted to move?" said Dylan.

"You worry about yourself, I kick arse on a regular basis with less rest than this," said Bruce.

A loud bang rang out as the offside front wheel blew out

and the steering pulled hard to the side. Bruce slammed the brakes on quickly to draw them to a halt.

"Fuck me, that's all we needed," said Bruce.

Dylan looked up ahead to the town, the edge of which was just a couple of hundred yards away now. It looked eerily quiet. A number of cars were parked up ahead as if nothing had happened. Had this sleepy little town remained oblivious to the world, or had the populace done a runner? It had to be one or another, because it was far too quiet for this time of day in any town. Dylan and Bruce watched as the shape of a person appeared in the distance. The two men were desperately trying to figure out whether the person was human or zombie.

"Mate, check the glove box, there should be some binoculars in there somewhere," said Bruce.

Dylan rooted through the pile of junk before pulling out a pair of compact binoculars.

"I suppose you use these for bird watching," asked Dylan.

"In the city, yeh. Give 'em here," said Bruce.

Dylan handed them to Bruce who held them up to look down the road. The person he was looking at was facing away from him, but turned whilst he was watching. The sight of a zombie's ugly face stared directly at him.

"Shit!" said Bruce

"Zombie?" asked Dylan.

"Yeh, let's get this wheel changed fucking asap!" said

Bruce.

The two men jumped out of the car.

"Connor, get that machinegun ready! Christian, keep an eye out all around, me and Dylan will get this wheel changed," said Bruce.

Connor hoisted the GPMG onto the roof of the car, slamming the heavy beast down on to the roof.

"Connor, watch the fucking paintwork!" said Bruce.

"What the fuck does that matter?" said Connor.

Bruce didn't even respond, knowing he was right, but not willing to accept the fact publically. He had loved the UTE's since he was a boy, and this was his absolute pride and joy. Christian jumped out and seized a rifle.

Bruce and Dylan grabbed the spare wheel, jack and wheel wrench from the tub. This would have to be the quickest wheel change they'd ever seen. Bruce shot a look up the street to see the number of zombies growing, a few already stumbling towards them. They must have some kind of group mentality.

"Should I shoot?" said Christian.

"If they get within a hundred yards, yes!" said Bruce.

He stuck the wrench onto the first nut and began loosening it off. Dylan slipped the jack under the car and wound it until it was firmly wedged between the floor and sill ready. By the time Bruce had got the first two nuts off the first zombie was already within the hundred yard range.

Christian fired off his first shot. The Steyr designed bullpup rifle fired the very accurate 5.56 NATO round. It was an exceptionally fine rifle in capable hands, but sadly Christian had never used anything but shotguns. His first shot missed the creature completely. He took better aim, the second shot hitting the shoulder of his target. The creature pulsated slightly with the hit, but it had no serious effect.

"Fuck sake, mate. Stop shooting like a girl, concentrate!" said Bruce.

Christian took a breath and held it to stop its effect on his accuracy. He aimed it dead centre to the creature's forehead and squeezed the trigger, textbook shooting as his father had always told him to do. The round hit the skull cleanly. The small rifle calibre showed barely any damage to its target, but the zombie collapsed dead to the ground.

"That's more like it!" said Connor.

The horde up ahead was now at least twenty zombies, and more were appearing from between buildings. Their number seemed to grow at an astonishing rate, as if the entire town was infected. This harsh reality crossed Bruce's mind, three hundred zombies and no working car. This was about as shit as situations come.

"Connor, get that thing shooting!"

He opened fire with the FN MAG. The sound was deafening for Bruce and Dylan working below, the odd bullet casing pinging off the plates of their armour. The 7.62 light machine gun packed a hell of a punch. Even the rounds that hit the torsos of the creatures were ripping them to shreds. It was unfortunate that they only had a hundred rounds for the gun. Bruce had got to the final nut but it was stuck. He stood up and stamped hard on the wrench several times until it finally came free.

"Dylan, get it jacked up!" said Bruce.

He lifted his new friend from the car, the Minimi. The horde was growing to uncontrollable levels now and Connor's FN was out. Holding the box fed machinegun at the waist, he opened fire on full auto. There was no time for clean kills and accurate shooting anymore. Connor and Christian joined his side with rifles and all three men fired away with everything they had. Blood splattered everywhere as clothes and flesh were ripped apart by the hail of bullets. Zombies were dropping dead every second, but their ammunition was reducing just as quickly.

Despite their best efforts and many kills, the unstoppable horde was now on them. Bruce passed the Minimi over to Connor and went back to Dylan. The car was jacked up but the wheel was seized to the brake and hub. Bruce kicked against the wheel, trying to break the seal.

The last rounds of the Minimi ran out and Connor and Christian ran back to the car to grab more ammunition for their rifles. The silence of the guns was one of the scariest and unpleasant moments all day. The only sound left was that of the groans from the evil horde and Bruce swearing whilst kicking the wheel.

The great sound of an old V8 turning over and firing up resounded in the background, perhaps only a few hundred yards in front of them in the town. So there was indeed life there. Bruce kicked the wheel hard enough that it freed up, but the power of the strike tipped the car from the jack sending the disc brake crashing to the ground.

"Fuck, fuck, fuck, fuck, shit, balls!" shouted Bruce.

They were now up shit creek without a paddle. The car could probably be brought back to life, but not with a bit of time to do so.

"Right, get some weapons, let's give these fuckers hell!" said Bruce.

Each of the men grabbed one of the AuSteyr rifles and formed a line. Had they got military training in firearms usage they could have perhaps had a chance of stopping the horde, but sadly, they didn't. They fired bursts off in an almost wild fashion. From behind the horde they could hear the roar of the V8 as several of the creatures turned around to investigate the threatening growl.

The survivors saw a rusty and battered old ford F150 power around a corner and appear behind the horde before them. Far from slowing down at the sight of the beasts, the truck stormed towards them at a hefty pace. The big chrome grill smashed into the mass of creatures sending them to the ground. Blood spewed up the bonnet, added to the dirt, dust and rust already decorating the old faithful workhorse.

The truck slid up alongside the survivors as the driver slammed on the old brakes, which could barely stop it. He was a man of about sixty, a rough old country man. A teenage girl was sitting beside him in the passenger seat with a Winchester underlever rifle.

"Get in!" the man shouted.

"Yes, sir! Dylan, Connor, grab the weapons and food from the car!" said Bruce.

The men hastily threw everything useful into the bed of the truck as the horde was just twenty feet away. Bruce jumped aboard as one of the zombies got within reach of the vehicle. He grabbed the flanged mace that lay next to him and swung at the beast's head.

"Have this you bastard!"

The mace smashed the skull just as the driver put his foot down and raced away. The men watched the bloodied creature tumble to the ground for the last time as they moved quickly into the distance. Bruce made his way to the front of the bed and the driver slid the rear window open.

"You're a life safer!" said Bruce.

"No, you are. The whole town had gone to shit and we had been trapped in our house for a day. It was only the ruckus that you caused that pulled those things away from us. We made a run for the truck whilst it was clear,"

he said.

"Well thank you, we helped you quite by accident, you could have left us to it," said Bruce.

"No worries, mate. We need your guns like you need our truck," said the man.

"Fair point, I'm Bruce, what's your name, mate?" asked Bruce.

"Jake, and this is Emily, my granddaughter, do you know what the hell is going on?" said Jake.

"Only what we've seen. There's some kind of infection out there, spread by biting, or maybe because of the shared bodily fluids. Everyone we've seen that's been bitten has become one of those things, which can only be described as zombies," said Bruce.

"Zombies? Don't bullshit me," said Jake.

"Well what else should we call them?" said Bruce.

The man shrugged his shoulders, it was a lot to take in, and he had no answers. The men in the truck bed were all silent. Connor handed out a bottle of water to each of the group from the supplies they'd found the day before.

"If you don't mind, son, how come you're wearing armour and carrying army rifles?" asked Jake.

"That's a fair point. We were doing an historical combat display when this all happened to us. We found the weapons earlier today," said Bruce.

"Found?" said Jake.

"The previous owners no longer had any use for them,"

said Bruce.

"If the army are incapable of surviving, then how are we?" asked Jake.

"We've managed so far, mate," said Bruce.

The man nodded in agreement, it at least provided some comfort to him.

"So where are we heading, Jake?" asked Bruce.

"To my sister's place."

"Whereabouts is it?" said Bruce.

"Just about twenty minutes drive," said Jake.

Bruce knew that the likelihood of the man's sister being alive was pretty slim, but it was a minor inconvenience to them, and he knew there was no way he could convince the man otherwise. Plus, the man had just saved all their arses, it was no time to argue. He sat back as comfortable as he could in the bed of the truck, with his back against the cab. His friends were all more than a little tired.

Bruce took this time to relax for the first time since this had all started. Since the outbreak he'd done little but fight and drive. Relaxing back on the hard floor, he sighed in relief as the cool air whistled through his hair. It was a lovely cooling effect. All the comfort that was lost by sitting in the hard metal truck bed was made up for by the freshening feeling of doing sixty miles an hour in the open air.

Ten minutes later Bruce was alerted by the sound of gunfire, two shots, one after the other. He stood up behind the cab to try and get a better view of things. The location of the gunfire was not yet in view. He knelt down to the window of the truck cab.

"That was shotgun fire," said Bruce.

Jake grinned and turned to Bruce.

"That'll be Paddy," said Jake.

The positivity of the man, as well as the continued evidence of more survivors, gave Bruce an immense feeling of hope. Despite enjoying some of the carnage he was able to dish out, he knew that life was going to become a whole lot more difficult before it got any easier.

If they could find three survivors in a matter of hours, then perhaps there were many more around the country and the world. For the first time he considered how lucky he'd been. This was a case of simply being in the right place at the right time, with the right clothing and the right friends. He turned around to his friends.

"Get ready, we're surely going into another shit storm," said Bruce.

The men grabbed their rifles and stretched out their aching limbs.

"Let me just say, you've all been good mates, we've got this far together," said Bruce.

None of the men replied, they were in shock to hear such sentimental words from their wise cracking and bad mouthing friend.

"Right, enough of this girly talk, let's kick some arse!"

he said.

Jake took a bend quickly, the tail end of the vehicle sliding on the dirt. The V8's power kept roaring as he didn't let up, steering with the gas pedal. The men in the back held on tight just to avoid being thrown out of the bed. A dozen zombies were in front of Paddy's house, perhaps more inside. Another shot rang out. It came from inside the house.

"Sorry to trouble you, mate, but we could really do with a hand here," said Jake.

"No problem, lets nail these fuckers," said Bruce.

Jake slammed the brakes on just thirty yards short of the front door and the wheels ground to a halt. The racket drew the attention of many of the zombies, who turned to look at the group with a blood lusting look.

Christian and Connor began laying down fire with their rifles whilst Bruce and Dylan leapt from the side to join the fight. They really had begun this fight far too close for comfort, Jake not thinking wisely about a plan of attack. The creatures were already stumbling towards them with more pouring from the house.

Bruce and his group opened up on full auto, panicked by the sudden realisation that they'd jumped out of the pan and into the fire. Jake had taken the under lever from his granddaughter and had joined the fight from his open door. Bruce's magazine, his last, had run out in seconds. He threw the gun down and pulled his poleaxe from the truck.

"Right, who wants some?" said Bruce.

The others' weapons were all empty before he could even take a few steps away from the truck bed. Bruce went forward as the others grabbed their steel from the vehicle. Holding the poleaxe in a high vertical guard, he swung the weapon down in a perfect diagonal cut to the closest creature's head. The metal poleaxe hammer smashed the skull in one blow, sending the body hurtling to the ground.

With the weapon head now resting on the ground, Bruce swung the weapon upwards with a back edge cut, the rear spike smashed into his second attacker's head. The rather large, blunt spike could not penetrate the head but it didn't matter, the blunt trauma knocked the creature off its feet. Walking up to the creature he hammered the bottom spike through the eye socket of the creature whilst it still lay on its back.

Bruce's friends had now got into action, hammering away with the big lumps of blunt steel they each had. The four armoured men were fighting in an utter bloodthirsty frenzy. The creatures were dropping all over the place and blood poured out over the ground. These hand-to-hand weapons were exceptional at fighting the slow, unarmed zombies. However, few people ever realise the biggest weakness of using these tools is fatigue.

After just two minutes, the men had killed thirty one zombies with a combination of rifle fire and hand weapons.

They were utterly exhausted, each man breathing heavily with sweat dripping from their dirty faces. Jake rushed though the smashed entrance of his sister's house.

"Paddy! Paddy?" called Jake.

"Jake, wait!" said Bruce.

He couldn't stop the man rushing into the house with an empty rifle. Bruce followed in after him.

"Dylan, stay here and keep watch!" said Bruce.

Getting to the stairs he found a partly demolished barricade leading to the upper floor. Jake was sat at the top of the stairs with his sister. Her shotgun was on the floor and she looked tired and pale.

"Jake? Is she ok?" said Bruce.

Getting closer to the woman he could already see clear signs of blood on her bare forearms. Bruce knew that this could be a very dangerous situation. Nobody wants to off a relative, especially when they're still living and breathing. At the same time, she could endanger more of the group. Not knowing what else to do, he jumped right in.

"Have you been bitten?" asked Bruce.

"Yes, by one of those foul things," said Paddy.

Jake shot a fearful look at Bruce, already suspecting what was coming next, but not wanting to accept it. He looked back to his sister.

"You know what this means, Jake," said Bruce.

"We need to bandage up these wounds Paddy, let's get you downstairs," said Jake.

"Jake!" shouted Bruce.

"What!" said Jake.

"What's all this fuss about? Stop shouting and start making some sense, both of you," said Paddy.

The two men looked at each other, neither fully agreeing with each other's hypothesis on the subject.

"Bruce here thinks that you're going to become one of those creatures because you've been bitten," said Jake.

She looked at her brother in shock. She'd put up a brave fight and had felt such relief to finally see her brother and be saved. All of the comfort she'd just felt was snatched away from her. She looked at Bruce with a long face.

"Is this true?" said Paddy.

"Yes, without a doubt, we've seen it too many times to think otherwise," said Bruce.

"But how can this happen?" said Paddy.

"We really don't know. Two days ago we were living our normal lives, and within minutes people were being bitten, dying, and getting back up and biting more people," said Bruce.

"So I will die from this?" said Paddy.

"Yes, you will stop breathing, die, and then come back to life as one of them," said Bruce.

"We don't know that for sure!" cried Jake.

"Yes we do. I don't know why or how, but we know for certain it will happen once you've been bitten by one of them," said Bruce.

"I don't want to live like that," said Paddy.

"No, it might not happen!" said Jake.

"You have trusted this man thus far, and he risked his life to save me, so I trust him," said Paddy.

The woman picked up the double barrelled shotgun that lay beside her and gave it to Jake.

"Please, make sure I never become one of those things," said Paddy.

"No, no, I can't do it, I won't!" screamed Jake.

"Then you would rather a stranger did it for you?" asked Paddy.

Jake looked up at her. The distinguished and tough old man had tears streaming down his face. He was not a coward or a weak hearted man in anyway, far from it, but this was most difficult thing ever in his life. He looked back at Bruce.

"Please, give us a minute," whispered Jake.

Bruce nodded, and walked out of the room. He went down the stairs and out the front door. His friends were sat about, weary from fighting.

As he came to a halt, a shot rang out, yet another survivor lost.

CHAPTER TEN

Bristol, England

It was pitch black and Zack was stood in the middle of the street. All around him was the rubbish and decay that had followed the zombie outbreak. Cars were abandoned, litter blew across the road and the many houses and businesses around him had been burnt or looted. It hadn't taken long for things to fall apart. None of this mattered though because Zack had a plan and right now a large group of the undead were blocking his route.

As the group reached him he calmly swung his ninja sword, killing a zombie with one swift cut. The edge of the razor sharp blade cut down through the skull and into the torso of the creature. He shouted out with joy as the blade literally cut the thing in half. Blood and gore sprayed over Zack but with no effect, other than to encourage him to strike another zombie in the same way.

Stood next to him were his best friends, each of them armed with an assortment of close quarter combat weapons and each dealing death in any direction the zombies came from. It was like they'd been doing this for years, it was a bloodbath and they were right in the middle of it.

"Holy shit, man! Did you see his arm come off?" laughed Max.

He wielded an evil looking two handed machete that had a series of spikes running down its back edge. He was in his early thirties and wearing a rough but sturdy looking leather jacket. The sound of laughter echoed from the others at the amusement of the situation.

"Come on, let's take the petrol station," shouted Tim, the third of the group.

Tim was already losing interest in the swirling melee and wanted something else. Another group of at least a dozen more zombies were heading towards them and Tim rushed forwards, hacking at them before the others could help in time.

"Tim you ass, stay with us!" shouted Zack.

The others stood watching, starting to get just a little annoyed at the idiot Tim who seemed to spend his life trying to lure them into stupid situations just for his own amusement.

"Follow me," he said as he disappeared through a

doorway.

The others were left out in the street with the sight of more zombies heading their way. Either they stood and fought or they followed Tim.

"Come on you noobs, this is a shortcut!" he shouted from a distance.

Max started to move towards the door and without even speaking followed after him. The doorway led into a shop front and then a dark and secluded looking corridor.

"I've got a bad feeling about this!" said Zack as they moved quickly through the building.

There was no sign of Tim until he started screaming at them from the other side of the building.

"Shit, they're all over me man, help me!" he screamed.

The other three rushed to him, finding his mutilated corpse on the ground and surrounded by at least a dozen zombies. Before they could turn to find a way out a loud wail from the horde announced they were trapped. Max pulled the door behind them, trying to hold them back but the creatures simply ripped through it and poured inside. There was only one other way out, a window at the side of the room. Zack tried to make his way across so that he could climb through but Tim managed to get in the way, too busy swinging his weapon to notice him.

"Stop wall blocking you noob!" cried Zack.

It was too late though. With no place to go and totally surrounded the three fought as hard and as fast as they could but it wasn't enough. After one too many bites it was over and one by one they fell. The computer screen faded to black with the familiar message of 'Game Over'.

Zack slumped back into his chair and sipped from a can of coke. He wore a loose pair of jeans, t-shirt and looked like he was in his mid teens. He certainly didn't looking anything like his gaming avatar!

"Tim, you're such a knob. You got us owned again. Next time, if you want to join our game you need to follow orders," said Zack in a dismissive tone.

Max started laughing, his voice coming over the voice communication software they were using.

He pressed a few keys on his keyboard as he took another swig from the can. Tim answered back, using his keyboard though rather than the voice communication. Zack leaned in closer, reading the small text, laughing as he read it.

"Stop bullshitting man, your cat didn't step on your keyboard."

Max continued laughing, his delayed crackling voice coming through the speakers. Almost as suddenly as it had started his laughter stopped, yet Zack could still just about hear his breathing. Listening carefully he was convinced he could hear Max's television set on.

"Max?" he asked.

"Holy shit, have you seen the news?" said Max, his

voice making Zack jump.

"Fuck me, Max, I thought you'd gone," laughed Zack.

The others two players didn't seem interested. Either that or they had simply found other more interesting things to do, so he carried on.

"According to this newsflash, the outbreak is getting worse. They think it's some kind of virus outbreak. They're saying people are turning on each other, biting and stuff," he added.

"That, my friends is why we've been staying low and gaming the last couple of days," said Zack. "When these kinds of epidemics start people can get a bit crazy. Just keep your heads down and order in more pizza!"

There was a pause for a short while as the friends considered Max's news.

"Hang on, biting, like zombies? Weird. Anyway, I'm gonna do some single player for a bit. Work on my tactics, you on later?" said the usually quiet Tim.

"Yeah, I'll be on later. Tim, you need the practice anyway, mate."

"What about the news?" asked Max.

"Who cares, it's probably just the bird flu or some other crap. The best thing if this is a really serious problem is to keep indoors. They said yesterday they thought it was a kind of flu. Stay in, eat pizza and game. Simple," said Zack.

"Good plan, though…isn't that always your plan?"

asked Max.

"So? Anyway, right now I need a bio break and then hopefully my bloody pizza will arrive. See you all back here in thirty minutes," answered Zack.

He removed his headset whilst he waited for their responses. The other player confirmed with the exception of the fourth one who had an unpronounceable name, due to all the special characters he'd used.

He left the computer and popped to the bathroom, still thinking about the fourth player. Either he was an insanely good gamer or more likely, he was a ten year old trying to act tough, thought Zack. Based on the last game though, he was almost certainly another noob. He might have felt their superior but Zack was only fifteen himself, though as far as he was concerned he was the best gamer out there and that meant he was the best, period. He washed his hands and then returned to his computer, his hunger now really starting to take hold.

"Bloody hell, I'm starving," he muttered to himself.

He opened up another window and checked on the status of his pizza. According to the screen it had been cooked and had been sent out for delivery over thirty minutes ago. The pizza place was only ten minutes walk away, even less by bike or car. Something must have gone wrong.

"Aw, shit!" he swore.

Thirty minutes meant at best a cold pizza and the only

thing Zack hated more than a cold pizza was team killers in online games. Those idiots were always turning up and spent all their time attacking their friends online. Anyway, forget them, he needed food and now. He clicked his mouse on the chat button to speak to one of the pizza representatives.

A window popped as somebody tried to offer assistance. Zack, feeling more than a little annoyed decided to get tough.

"Where's my pizza?" he typed, muttering as he hit the keys.

The window was static for a short while before letters appeared, presumably by one of the pizza staff. It simply said, 'hhelp us' and was then followed by lots of random characters. Even the word help was misspelt.

Zack was not in the mood. His stomach ached and he needed his pizza fix. He sent several more messages but nothing came back. This was weird, the pizza place was usually quick and their chat facility had always worked in the past. As he sat there thinking about alternatives to the pizza shop he heard what sounded like a car crash.

"What the hell!" he exclaimed.

Walking over to his window he pulled back the curtains and look out. His flat was on the sixth floor, but even from here he could make out the crashed car. It looked like a saloon and was wedged between two parked cars. It must have lost control and skidded off the road. As he watched he saw a group of people trying to help the passenger. There was a scream and a number of them ran away, one being dragged to the ground by the occupants. From where he stood it looked like they were biting those on the ground.

Staying where he was he pulled his Smartphone from his pocket and checked the news application. It confirmed what Max had said. He looked back out, then the pangs of hunger kicked in again. The problem was that he'd already paid for his pizza online and he had no more money left until his parents came home tomorrow. Also, what the hell was going on at the pizza place? Maybe they needed his help. Yeah, they needed his help!

Zack hit the speed dial key to Max.

"Hey, Max," he said.

"Sup Zack, thought you were on a break?" answered Max.

"Yeah, I was but I think this outbreak might be bigger than we thought. I keep trying to call the pizza place, nobody's replying. Even crazier though, I sent them a chat message on their website and they just said 'help us!' What the fuck is going on?" he asked.

"Tell me about it. I got a call from my Dad to say he's stuck at the hospital. He said they're getting loads of people coming in. He won't be back until the morning," said Max.

Zack moved back to his computer, loading up his

internet browser and checking different websites for more information.

"I'm checking online, you think this could be serious?" asked Zack.

One of the stories caught his eye. It linked to a video clip of a situation in northern Spain. He clicked on it and watched it, to his excitement it was almost a mirror of the game they'd been playing. Max started to answer him but Zack interrupted him with his excitement.

"Holy shit! This is fucking awesome. Get on your PC, I'll send you this link," he said.

There was a bit of noise at the other end as Max presumably returned to his computer. A chat window popped up and Zack pasted in the internet address to the video clip. He could hear it playing on Max's computer through the phone. As Max watched it, Zack hit the replay button on his own computer and watched the action again. It looked like an outdoor theatre of some kind. There was a stage and circular, raised seating most of the way around it, like an ancient Odeon. The spectators were screaming and trying to get away from the place. Some ran, others climbed over the hurt. It was a mad panic.

As some of the people ran past the camera a person stepped into shot, grabbing at one of those running by. The attacker was a middle-aged man but there was something strange but familiar about him. There was blood dripping from his mouth, his flesh was pale and he moved with a ridged, uncomfortable gate. As he grabbed hold of the person he lunged forwards, biting into the woman's shoulder and then pulled her down to the ground. As the two people dropped down another two similar people knelt down and joined in, literally feeding on the dying woman.

"Fuck me!" came down the line from Max, "Are you thinking what I'm thinking?" he asked.

"Zombies!" said Zack.

"Yeah!" agreed Max, "fucking zombies and it looks like it's already underway. This is awesome! I knew we did all this gaming for a reason, it was for today!"

"Fuck, yeah!" said a grinning Zack, "Get Tim online, we need to put out seventy two hour plan into action. You still got your paperwork?"

"You're kidding right? Ever since you got that How to Survive a Zombie Apocalypse book I've had everything ready for this day. He's here," said Max.

With all three of them in front of their computers they switched to their headsets so they could discuss their plan as a group.

"Okay Tim, it looks like this is the Zompoc," said Zack.

"Holy shit! You're kidding me?" asked Tim.

"No shit, this is the real deal. We need to check, there's no point putting the plan into action unless this is for real. My plan is we meet up at The Mall. It's on the main road and the out of town retail stores are there," said Zack.

With a few key presses Zack loaded up a map of the town, tracing the route he would need to reach the retail park. The site was big but away from most people. It wasn't perfect but it was in a much better area than where Tim and Max lived in the centre of the town and offered them options, something the town did not.

"Yeah, we need to hit those retail places for our equipment," agreed Tim.

"We need to get going and fast if this is anything like the movies we'll be overrun in hours. It might already be too late; we've been gaming for hours whilst this shit has been going down. We need to get out, get equipped, supplied and safe before this place goes to shit," said Max.

"Ok, sounds like a plan. I'm going to get to Max's flat, he's only a few streets from here. We'll then meet you at the railway bridge outside town. From there we'll get to the retail park. We'll meet in thirty minutes," said Zack.

With the plan ready to go Max and Tim both disconnected, leaving Zack on his own. Still hungry but also a little excited. He opened his cupboard and grabbed his 'bug out' bag though he couldn't remember what he'd actually put in it.

After the hours of discussion with his friends at school he'd gone and made a day based plan and even started to hoard equipment, just in case it was needed. He threw on his jacket and then went out to the kitchen, grabbing a few more cans of coke to keep him going. His stomach groaned, instantly reminding him that he needed food and fast. Checking his watch the time was just past eleven o'clock. Not a problem usually for pizza delivery but a big problem for finding stores that were still open.

The last things he grabbed were his phone and keys. Opening the front door carefully he peeked out into the hallway, all seemed clear. He locked the door and then made his way to the lift. The building was surprisingly quiet and he started to wonder that maybe not leaving the flat for the last thirty six hours might now be a problem. What if a zombie apocalypse had started the day before? According to all the books and films he'd seen, this is the time when things got really bad.

Jumping in the lift he hit the button and waited for the doors to close. As always, when he was in a hurry nothing seemed to happen. After a short pause though, the door slid shut and his descent started. He considered the map he'd been looking at before he left. Max's place was across the road and then three streets behind it, just before the pizza place.

The lift pinged and the doors slid open to reveal the lobby. It was the nicest part of the apartment complex, with marble walls and the mailbox lockers on one side. He opened the secure door and stepped into the street. It was just as it looked from upstairs, just louder and somehow less safe. To one side was the crashed car and he was sure he could see people, probably bodies in the street. Behind the car was a group of at least thirty people staggering around. Either they were all drunk or they were Zack's first look at a real world zombie. He ducked down behind a parked Volvo and looked around, making sure his route was ok. From his position it looked like the only group was to the left.

Throwing caution to the wind, and feeling a sense of danger and a little excitement, he launched himself from behind the car and rushed across the street. In just a couple of seconds he was on the pavement at the other side and continued walking away from his home. Taking the side road he stayed on the pavement and carried on walking, without noticing anything untoward. Cars were parked in the street as normal but there didn't seem to be many cars actually driving around. As he reached the corner he could make out the building where Max lived on the opposite corner. Max was a little older and shared with several other university students.

After years of gaming he knew only too well the dangers that unknown streets and corners offered. He moved out into the road but kept his head down to avoid attention. As he crept forward he noticed some more of the zombie-like people in an alley to the left. He stopped and watched for a moment, it looked like they were robbing a third person. He was about to shout when he saw them biting into the man's flesh.

"Holy fuck!" whispered Zack to himself.

He continued his slow movement to the street corner where Max lived. It was an old stone townhouse with three storeys and a basement that the students often used for late night parties. The windows on the ground floor were flashing and the dull thud of the bass from a powerful sound system made the old Victorian window panes vibrate.

A series of groans emanated from across the street. At first Zack thought it was from the creatures in the alley but he quickly spotted a group of dozens more in the street. He looked in the other three directions and his suspicions were confirmed, the zombies were being drawn to the sound and possibly the lights of the house. Zack looked at the other buildings, but none were producing the sound or light that could possibly get so much attention.

Taking a deep breath he hurled himself the last short distance and started banging on the heavy wooden door. There was no reply, probably because of the extremely loud noise. He looked back over his shoulder to see the horde in the street was getting closer. The only good thing was that they were moving at a very slow pace. He turned back to the door to find a man stood in front of him. Zack staggered backwards, shocked by the appearance of the man.

"What's up, kid?" asked a man in his late twenties.

Waiting a moment to catch his breath, Zack stepped up closer to the man.

"I'm not a kid," said Zack indigently, "I'm here to see Max."

"Whoa, tough guy!" laughed the man as he beckoned Zack inside. Without pausing Zack was inside and made sure the door was shut behind him.

The sound in the hallway was insanely loud, it sounded like they were playing Wheels of Steel again on their Rock Band game. He moved into the room to the sight of four men and a couple of women smoking and drinking. Three of the men and one of the women were playing fake guitars and drums, whilst an older man in his thirties slaughtered the song with his out of tune voice. For some reason, whenever they played this game they just had to choose the never ending version of the Saxon song. One of the men hammered like crazy on the set of imitation drums and the final man, stripped to the waist was strumming away on his plastic guitar. There were at least two more of the group, who were either asleep or passed out, and there were cans and fast-food boxes everywhere. It was so sad to Zack, these games were for children and pensioners, gamers didn't play this kind of crap.

As Zack stood watching them playing at being in a band Max appeared. He was wearing a thick coat and carried a bag on his back. Max looked older than Zack and more like the other members of the house than the pale faced Zack. He shouted something to him but the noise was too great.

Zack stepped over to the speakers and without pausing hit the power button. The sound dropped off almost instantly, though the rest of the band members continued singing or hitting away at their instruments. In just seconds the room was in uproar. The older man on the microphone launched into a tirade.

"What the fuck are you doing you stupid little prick?" he screamed.

"Haven't you seen outside, there are zombies and you're attracting them here with your noise?" said Zack.

The man playing the drums stood up, walking towards Max.

"You're fucking kidding me? Your friend taking the piss?" he swore.

Max stepped between Zack and the man.

"He's not kidding, there's some kind of outbreak going on, haven't you seen the news?"

One of the women staggered over with a glass of cheap wine in her hand.

"Who cares?" she muttered, "they can join in if they want!"

Zack interjected, "Come on people, listen to yourselves. There's some serious shit going on out there. We need to get out of here."

"Shut up, tough guy," laughed one of the others as he returned to the sound equipment.

"Max, if you want to go, go, otherwise leave us in

peace," said the man.

He leaned down and pushed the lead back in, the music kicked back in almost deafening Zack. The rest of the revellers moved back to their seating or instruments and continued where they'd left off.

Max signalled to Zack to follow him. The two made for the kitchen area that was at the back of the house. Though the sound was deafeningly loud they could just about hear each other.

"Zack, you're sure this is the real deal?" asked Max.

"You bet! I've checked all the news sites, video feeds, the lot. The shit has hit the fan right across the world. If we wait much longer we'll never get out," he said.

They were interrupted by the flickering of the lights. With just two flashes the lighting in the house was cut. There was a lot of shouting from the group around the band equipment though the music still kept playing. Max and Zack stepped back into the room, wary of what might lurk in the darkness. A shape moved passed them and they both watched it carefully. As their eyes adjusted to the light they noticed it was the drummer, he disappeared into the hallway. Zack looked around, checking for any sign of the zombies. So far it looked like they were okay.

With a flash the lights came back on, the man must have left the room to flick the trip on the consumer unit. There was no sign of him though and this concerned Zack. The man on the microphone shouted over the speakers for the drummer to come back and get in the game.

From the hallway the drummer emerged, but to the shock of Zack and Max he was covered in blood. Taking just a few steps he staggered into the room and then collapsed. One of the women screamed, the rest dropped their instruments and ran over to the wounded man. Max stood in disbelief and finally believed that something bad was really happening. Zack on the other hand ran straight for the door where the drummer had come from. He threw he weight against the door and swung it shut just as a bloodied arm pushed through the gap. He tried to shout to the others for help, but the Saxon song kept on pounding away. The arm waved around trying to grab at Zack. He turned to Max but he was still stood there, doing nothing. Zack waved at him, trying to draw his attention. Finally Max snapped out of it and grabbing the nearest thing he could find, a DVD box set of Dirty Harry films. He ran forward, smashing the box down on the hand. It loosened its hold and the two of them were able to force the door shut.

Zack slid the door's bolt across, sealing the room, at least for now. Whilst Max stood watching the unfolding scene, Zack ran across the room and pulled the cable on the music. With the sound gone it was replaced by groans from the injured drummer. A large puddle of blood expanded across the floor and it was obvious to most of them that he was going to die. A woman screamed, whilst the others tried to stem the flow of blood from the hurt man. The two, who until now had been sleeping or more likely passed out, were forced awake by the shrill scream. The drummer started to shake, blood spurting from his mouth before finally laying still.

"Fuck!" shouted the Tony, the oldest of the group.

"Is he dead?" screamed the drunken Naomi.

"Of course he's dead," shouted Tony, "look at the fucking holes in his body!"

He turned to look at Zack, "Did those fucking zombie things do this?"

Zack backed off, sensing danger from this man.

"Probably, why don't you look outside?" he suggested.

"Yeah, maybe I will!" he shouted.

Leaving the body of their friend on the ground, Tony walked over to the large bay window that looked overlooked the street. There were two large curtains currently pulled across it to keep passersby from looking in. As the rest of the group continued talking he ripped open the curtains to reveal the full bay window. At every pane of glass was a bloodied and pale face.

"Fuck!" shouted Tony as he stumbled backwards, falling onto his back.

Laura, the woman who had been screaming was hiding in the corner of the room, muttering to herself, obviously scared to death by what she'd seen.

John, one of the men that had being playing the guitar

knelt down to the wounded drummer.

"Have you seen this?" he asked.

The rest followed his gaze as he pointed out the wounds on the man. There were what looked like bite and chew marks on his neck, shoulder, waist and arm.

"He was only out there for a few seconds. What animal would attack like that?"

"Look, people!" shouted Zack as loudly as he could.

"I've already told you. There's some kind of outbreak going on and they're attacking the living. That's you and me. We can't stay here. You need to get out of town, that's what me and Max are doing."

The door to the hallway started shaking as the creature tried to force its way inside. Tony ran up to the bay window and closed the curtains, covering the windows. He then turned back, giving a forced grin, and moved to the wall socket pulling the plug on the sound system, finally quieting the room.

"I can't take looking at them anymore," he said in a matter of fact tone.

With the music now gone they could all hear the hammering and battering sounds from scores or maybe even hundreds of the monsters trying to work their way in.

The glass shattered and the curtains were quickly ripped down. Tony turned to see dozens of the creatures forcing their way through the smashed glass windows. Almost simultaneously the door to the hall ripped open and a number of zombies staggered into the front room. These two groups now surrounded the revellers in the large room. To their front was the smashed bay window, to one side was the broken door to the hallway and at the back of the room was another door that led into the kitchen. Steve, one of the guitarists, tried to escape from the room but was caught by the first zombie in the corridor and thrown up against the wall.

Naomi started screaming again, whilst the others panicked and each doing what they thought was best in the situation. Tony lifted the drum and its cheap metal stand and swung it at the first creatures coming into the room. The other men grabbed the guitar and microphone stand and joined in, smashing and striking at the zombies at the bay window.

"Get this fucking thing off me!" screamed Steve.

Zack and Max attempted to help the man at the wall who was trying to avoid being bitten. As the three struggled with the tall zombie even more poured in from the corridor.

Naomi, still screaming simply drew attention to herself by her noise and was soon dragged down by three zombies. She reached out, grabbing the only item that was on the floor, it was the remote control for the television. She lifted it and swung it hard into the face of one of the zombies. It knocked the creature to the side but it was quickly back and bit into her hand forcing her to drop it. She opened her mouth to cry for help but another zombie climbed over her and bit down into her throat, tearing out a mouthful of flesh. As the blood gushed from the wound she made one final effort to throw the closest one off her, but it was too late. With the massive trauma to her body she passed out and it was probably for the best as more of the zombies joined in the feeding frenzy.

Laura, who was still delirious from whatever she had been drinking or eating previously, staggered to the corridor with a fire poker in her hands that she must have grabbed from the fireplace. She may have been as drunk as Naomi, but she had no intention of simply screaming and then dying. Two more zombies entered the room from the corridor and screaming loudly she rushed at the first one, stabbing hard with the weapon. With little effort the heavy lump of metal smashed into the creature's chest and impaled it on the door. Even as it lay pinned it kept moving, trying to bite and snap at her. On the shelf next to the door was a lamp. She grabbed it and smashed it hard on the zombie's head. The lamp smashed into pieces and yet the zombie still wouldn't die.

"Die, you fuck!" screamed Laura as she grabbed onto the poker and pulled at it. With one final tug she managed to pull it from the zombie's body and without hesitating she stabbed again but this time at its head. With one swift motion it penetrated the front of the head and smashed out through the rear of the thing's skull. It collapsed lifelessly in front of her. Another zombie tried to grab her but she ducked under its arms and kicked at its leg. The brittle bone snapped at the knee and it fell to the ground near the skewered zombie.

The final zombie from the corridor staggered towards her. Now seriously pissed off she bent down and placed her boot onto the skewered zombies head. With a tug the poker pulled out. Holding it like a baseball bat she swung the heavy wrought iron tool and managed to strike it in the head, caving in its skulls and dropping it to the ground. The weight and mass of the tool however swung it off to her right and ended up embedded in the wall, narrowly missing Zack and Max in their struggle with the tall zombie. As she tried to retrieve the weapon another zombie appeared and forced her back into the room. She retreated to a small table covered in large potted plants.

Steve was pinned to the wall and was using all his strength to hold off the tall zombie. Every few seconds it snapped its jaws, trying to take chunks out of him. Max, being the bigger and stronger of the two managed to pull it off Steve. As the zombie staggered backwards Zack looked around for a weapon. The closest thing to him was the television unit. It was too big for him to use effectively so he grabbed the next closest thing, the Playstation 3 console sitting on the shelf next to it. Pulling it out of its alcove the cables dropped from the rear. It was about as big as a flattened shoebox and weighed a few kilos. Lifting it above his head he brought it down hard onto the zombie's head, the creature dropped to its knees. With one more swing he connected with the zombie's jaw and sent it flying into the television set.

"Bloody hate consoles!" he shouted.

Max grinned at him as he grabbed a world atlas from the bookshelf and smashed it into the face of another. The zombie's feet came up, almost as though he'd done a wrestling clotheslines move. As it lay on its back Zack stepped in and issued the coup de grace with the console. Back in the front of the room the small group led by Tony were still smashing away with their instruments at the zombies. The guitar was already broken into pieces and one of the zombies lay shaking on the ground with a drum around his head. The group were fighting their way back towards the rear of the house. Laura was armed with what looked like a large terracotta flower pot. She smashed it onto a zombie and then ran, dodging the outstretched arms of at least a dozen zombies to almost reach where Max was stood. With just a few feet to go she tripped over a fallen zombie, landing hard on her left arm. She howled in pain, possibly breaking the arm in the fall.

Looking at the rear of the house Zack could see the path through to the kitchen was clear. It was their only way out as more zombies were forcing their way into the rest of the house.

"Come on!" shouted Zack, though only Max seemed to be paying him any attention.

Zack grabbed the woman's right arm and started dragging her to the kitchen. Max joined in, desperate to get out of the room that was now swarming with the undead. Zack and Max were already almost at the door to the kitchen before Tony spotted them. One of his friends was dragged down, bitten and torn at by zombies. Lifting up a cushion from the sofa he held it in front of him and simply ran, barging zombies out of the way. One tried to block his path so he thrust the cushion at its face, jamming it inside the creature's mouth and then punched the cushion repeatedly. With its mouth blocked he was able to smash it back until he could move past it. Steve was still on the floor and seeing the attempted escape quickly got up and chased after Max.

"Hey, where the fuck are you going?" shouted Tony.

Max turned briefly to shout back.

"We said we're going and we are. Join us or stay here," he said as he disappeared into the kitchen.

Tony followed and just as he reached the kitchen doorway more glass shattered, revealing yet more of the things making their way into the house. The entire front room was now packed with creatures. Anybody still left was either dead or soon would be. With a last look Tony rushed into the kitchen and slammed the door shut behind him. Inside stood Steve, Laura, Zack and Max, stunned speechless by the recent events.

"Where are the others?" asked Max.

"Gone, they're all gone," said a stupefied Tony.

"Look, like I said. If we stay here we'll die. There are too many of them, we need to get away from people and find somewhere safe. We're going to The Mall," said Zack.

"Mall?" asked Steve.

"Yeah, you know, in the retail park, near the cinema," said Max.

Steve nodded in acknowledgement. The door started shaking, the zombies evidently trying to make their way into the kitchen to finish the job.

"Come on, follow me," said Zack.

He opened the back door and led the small group out into the back yard. The yard was quite small and had a large eight foot high wall all around it. There was a large shed right at the back and a tree next to it. As they stepped out the exterior light flicked on, alerted by their presence.

"Great," muttered Tony.

"Won't that draw more of those things to us?" said Laura, as she pointed at the light.

"No shit!" answered Steve sarcastically.

In the distance the sound of shouting and screaming could be heard, along with the sound of house alarms and the emergency services.

"I told you, this place is going to hell," said Zack.

He climbed the lowest branch of the tree and lifted himself onto the top of the flat roofed shed. Max followed him and from their raised position they had a much better view of the area. From the shed they could climb down the wall and into the street or they could drop the other side into the neighbour's garden. Out in the distance Zack could see an orange glow. He concentrated, trying to work out exactly what it was.

"Holy shit!" he exclaimed as he worked out what was going on.

"What?" asked Laura.

"The flats three streets down are on fire and there are people fighting in the street near it," said Zack.

Max turned back to the other three, gesturing to the wall.

"Look, we're going to take the lane that way," he gestured off to his left, "and then over the fence to follow the railway line. We'll take it till we get to the bridge."

"And then?" asked Tony.

"Then we'll be at the retail park and can get supplies and dig in."

Laura moved to the tree, offering up her hand. Max and Zack helped her up whilst Tony and Steve watched.

"I'm going with them, you coming?" she asked.

Before an answer was required the door to the rear of the house smashed open and three zombies staggered out.

"Fuck!" shouted Steve.

They both found instant motivation to climb up onto the shed and in seconds all five were ready. Zack, knowing the area best moved off first. The drop from the shed was only a few feet and easily achieved. With him and Max down they helped Laura though the other two men refused help, climbing down and starting to move off ahead of the group. They crossed the street and turned down the dark, unlit lane that led to a field. At one time it had been a popular sports field used for rugby and football. These days it was rough and unkempt, used only for dog walking.

The group of five followed a rough trail towards the woodland. Zack and Max led, making quick progress to the perimeter of the woodland. As they entered it the amount of light reduced and progress became more difficult and slower. Tony moved up to the front, questioning Zack.

"Why are we going this way? High Street is a much quicker way than this," said Tony.

Zack said nothing, he was too busy concentrating on checking his immediate area for problems.

"Quicker, if you want to die, yeah. We need to stay away from people. People and zombies are always in the same place. Haven't you ever seen Dawn of the Dead?" asked Max.

"Is that the one with the train?" asked Laura.

"Uh, no. It's the one where a small group escape the city to take refuge in a shopping mall," said Max.

"Yeah, I know that one," said Steve, "They try and

escape in trucks at the end, right?"

"Exactly," said Max, "and that's why we're getting out of this populated area and into somewhere that's low on people and high in safe places with supplies and weapons."

Zack moved out of the woodland and into the open, finally seeing the embankment ahead that led to the railway line. He climbed through a small hole in the wire fencing and then turned to helped Max and the rest through.

"We need to follow the line to the right, it will lead us out of town," he said.

It took a little while for all five of them to climb through. After a couple of minutes they were all at the top of the embankment and walking parallel with the railway line. As they walked they were granted a wide panoramic view of the town and the immediate area around it. Usually at this time you'd expect to see nothing but the orange glow from urban light pollution, but tonight there were all manner of lights. As well as the street and building lighting there were the flashing red and blue of the police as well as the fire brigade and a large number of ambulances. From the skyline at least four fires were burning, two of which were massive conflagrations.

"Looks like the bloody blitz, mate," said Tony.

"Yeah," answered Steve, "do you reckon any of the others got out alive?"

Tony turned his head with a look of despair on his face. He simply didn't know what to say. It was hardly surprising, when just minutes before he'd watched some of his closest friends be torn apart right before his eyes.

In the front Max was trying to use his phone to call his family and not doing well. The phone showed a strong signal yet refused to connect.

"I can't connect," he said.

"Yeah, it's probably because everybody else is trying to use their phones. Maybe try again later," said Zack.

Laura moved up to speak with Zack.

"How much further to the bridge?" she asked.

Zack looked back, checking roughly how far they had travelled.

"We're about halfway to the bridge, so about five more minutes," he said.

"How do you know so much about these zombies?" asked Laura.

"Me, Max and some of our friends are really interested in zombie games and films. Always have been," he explained.

"Zombie games, like video games?" she asked.

"Well, computer games. We like playing first person shooters mainly," he said.

Laura looked a little confused though it was hardly unexpected. Zack found he received the same expression from most people when he mentioned playing certain computer games. He reached into his bag and pulled out several books. He handed her the largest one, it was white and showed various people with weapons on the front. She held it up so that the orange glow from the town lit up its pages.

"How to Survive a Zombie Apocalypse, are you for real?" she asked.

Zack laughed, "Yeah, real serious. That book is what saved our lives. Hiding in an urban area is a big problem. If you think about it you'll find it's all common sense stuff."

Laura said no more, she was intrigued by several of the illustrations and yet was confused by the bizarre nature of the book. Turning to the rest of the group she showed the book to Tony.

"Have you seen this book?" she asked him.

Tony glanced at the title, spotting the familiar white cover.

"Yeah, Max is always going on about it. Why?" he asked.

"Well, it might be a good idea to have a look at it if we get a chance," she said.

Moving back up to Zack she spoke to him again, "Mind if I borrow this?"

Zack considered her question for a moment, not completely happy giving up the book but then also conscious of the fact that he knew it from cover to cover.

"Sure, just don't lose it," he said as he smiled.

Max moved closer to Zack and interrupted his

conversation with Laura.

"So we get out of town and get to the retail park. Then what?" he asked.

Laura turned back to speak with the others whilst Max and Zack continued their discussion.

"Well, at the park we've got The Mall, supermarket and loads of out of town stores. I suggest we choose the one with the most supplies and easiest to defend and occupy. Also, we need one with options in case we need to escape in a hurry," said Zack.

"Oh yeah, not like the gun shop in the Dawn of the Dead remake right?" said Max.

"Exactly," answered Zack. "The only options he had were the roof or the door. We need lots of options in case something unexpected happens."

The group reached a small stone wall running parallel with the track. Tony stepped closer, looking down the embankment.

"Is this it?" he asked.

Max scrambled down the steep embankment till he reached the darkness below. He was quiet for a moment, presumably looking around at the road and area below for signs of trouble.

"Looks ok," he called.

The rest of the group climbed down with Tony and Steve gave Laura a hand on the slippery grass. Once they reached the bottom they looked around at the dark location. The lights seemed to be not working for some reason. Luckily the glow from the distant town partially lit the road. To their right the main road went back into town. There were no vehicles on it from what they could see and only a couple of detached houses dotted the road over a distance of around a mile. In the opposite direction the road passed under the railway bridge to a cross roads and then continued off into the distance. The left turn on the crossroads simply went to a gate that led to a railroad storage area. The right turn was one of the entrances to the large shopping park. On the road was a large sign displaying a map of the site. In the centre was a large mall, surrounding this was a series of circular roads leading to other large department stores and a massive supermarket.

Max moved across the road and checked both sides carefully. He looked confused and a little worried.

"What's wrong?" asked Laura.

Max continued looking whilst Zack checked back on the road leading into town. Laura followed him, repeating her question.

Tim, our friend Tim is supposed to be meeting us here. He only lives a few minutes away.

Maybe he's already gone to The Mall?" she asked.

"Maybe," he answered.

Max wandered back over to them.

"No sign of him," he said is a miserable tone.

Tony and Steve crept up, listening to the conversation.

"We can't wait here. If he made it we'll find him, if not then tough!" said Tony.

"Tough?" shouted Max as he swung for Tony.

Luckily Zack grabbed him at the last minute and pulled him back.

"Come on, Tony's right, even if he's acting like an ass. We need to keep moving. We're no good to anybody if we get caught out here," said Zack.

Max nodded uncomfortably, knowing too well he was right. After one final check Zack moved under the railroad bridge and crossed the road, heading directly for the entrance to the retail park. The others waited for a moment before crossing and following him.

"Are we going to The Mall then?" asked Steve.

"Yes, we need to do a quick recce of the area and much sure it's clear first. The ideal places are the supermarket and The Mall itself. The Mall would be best to start with and we can raid the supermarket over the next few days," replied Zack.

The group kept moving whilst Tony started ranting.

"Next few days! What the fuck? I thought we were gonna be here for just a few hours until this thing blows over," he said.

Max started to laugh and Zack turned his head in amusement.

"I don't think you realise what's going on, Tony," said Zack sarcastically.

"This is just the start. The first few days will be hard. If we survive we'll need to get supplies for the next days, weeks and maybe even months."

"Fuck!" shouted Tony.

As they rounded the next corner they were greeted with the distant silhouette of the closed retail park. The closest structure was to the right and consisted of a large car wash and petrol station. Another few hundred yards further down the road was a large block of warehouse type stores. Beyond the stores was the massive structure of The Mall. Like most modern malls it contained as many stores as a small town.

"There it is," said Laura as she pointed in the distance.

The group increased speed until a hand gesture from Zack made them all stop. Tony moved forwards, about to say something when Max pounced on him, pushing his hand over the man's mouth.

"Sshhhh," he whispered.

He gestured for Tony to duck down with him. As they dropped down Steve spotted what was concerning him and quickly pulled Laura off to the right and into cover. As the five of them stayed low they watched the scene ahead. Zack had been the first to spot the overturned double-decker bus. It was off the road and embedded in the tree line. For whatever reason, the bus had ended up on its side with part of the roof and side ripped off.

What really got their attention though was the large

group of bodies and people milling around the crash site. At least thirty or forty of them were staggering around, almost certainly zombies. On the road and pavement were the bodies of another dozen more, probably those that had tried to escape. Whether the zombies caused the crash or came after the crash wasn't clear. What was important though, was that this group of zombies stood between the petrol station and the shopping mall.

"Can we go around?" said Max.

"Nah, if we leave them they could maybe find a way into The Mall or even let others know we're there. We need to get rid of them," said Zack firmly.

Steve heard what he was saying and crept up closer.

"What the fuck are you talking about, little man? This isn't one of your games. We've got no weapons and there are only four of us plus you," he said sarcastically.

Zack turned his hand, swearing to himself. He didn't want to stay in this exposed position for any longer than they had to. If a zombie spotted them they would be in big trouble. Whilst he considered what to do Steve grabbed Laura's arm and started pulling her to the left of the road.

Max tried to stop him but he pushed the man back and kept moving forwards.

"What the hell is he doing?" said Zack.

Max held up his hands in disgust.

"No idea man, looks like he's gonna do a Leroy to us,"

he said.

Steve and Laura appeared to be having an argument, it was quite clear that she didn't want to go with him. With a final push she forced herself away, leaving Steve exposed on his own, out in the open. Laura ran back to take cover with the others whilst Steve turned on them with a verbal tirade.

"Listen man, those things killed our friends. If we go off half-cocked we'll join them," he pleaded.

"Yeah, true but if we turn back we'll be out in the open with just these for weapons," said Max as he held out half a brick he'd just found.

"Fuck this!" said an angry Tony, "I can't believe I'm saying this but I agree with Zack. He's been right so far and if we can get in The Mall we'll have food, clothes, weapons and a safe place to hole up. I say we take them and take them now before anymore show up."

"Yeah!" said a satisfied Max.

Tony turned back to Zack, showing him perhaps a little of the respect his normally reserved for his friends like Steve.

"Okay, little fella. What's your plan?" he asked.

Zack scratched his chin as he looked around.

"We've got no weapons so we're going to have to find something to use as a weapon," he said.

"No shit!" said Steve.

The group looked around until the silence was broken

by Laura.

"The petrol station, would they have weapons?" she asked.

"Nah," said Steve, "just petrol."

"Petrol! That's brilliant!" said Zack, "Do any of you have a light?"

Steve, Laura and Tony reached into their pockets and fished out three lighters almost simultaneously.

"Just like buses!" laughed Max.

What's your plan?" asked Tony.

Zack took one of the lighters and proceeded to look around, checking on the location. He paced forwards and backwards a few steps until he had something concrete in mind.

"Ok, try this. We use the fuel at the station to burn the whole lot of them. It's quick and guaranteed to work," said Zack.

"Great plan you idiot," retorted Steve, "how are you going to burn them all when they're so far away?"

"Yeah, I see where you're going with this," said Max, "you're thinking of the exploding petrol station in Left 4 Dead right?"

Zack grinned in acknowledgment.

"Steve has a point though," continued Max, "we need something like the beeping pipe bomb to get them all in one place."

"Pipe bomb?" asked Laura.

Steve turned away, waving his hands in the air as he muttered.

"No, you don't get it. In the game the pipe bomb makes a noise and has a flashing light. It attracts the zombies so they can all be killed together," explained Max.

Tony seemed to be following what he was saying and called over to Steve.

"Hey, Steve," he called in the quietest but firmest voice he could manage. He turned to Max and Zack.

"You're talking about bait right?" he asked.

"Exactly!" answered Zack.

A rustling sound came from ahead and forced them all into silence. Steve ducked back down into cover, his fear of the zombies outweighing his desire to stay away from the least significant of their group. They watched carefully as a small number of the zombies split off from the crash scene and staggered down the road towards them.

"Aw crap!" said Max.

"Look, we haven't got much time. We need to get to the station!" shouted Zack.

He grabbed Laura's arm and pulled her in the direction of the petrol station. Max and Tony quickly followed, leaving just Steve who refused to move. They rushed off down the short road that followed a shallow gradient. Tony kept checking over his shoulder for Steve but there was no sign of him. As they reached the station they first went to the payment booth. It was closed and securely locked against break-ins or theft.

"Shit!" shouted Tony.

"Look!" called Laura as she pointed up the hill.

Steve emerged from the crest of the hill, running as fast as he could. Tony turned to Max but before he could speak Max shouted.

"Look, they're after him."

Up on the hill the first group of zombies appeared, each staggering down the hill and after Steve.

"I don't know what he did, but they've taken the bait!" said Max.

At the payment booth Zack was trying to pick the lock but with no success. The doors and windows were protected by heavy steel shutters and then fitted with several tubular locks.

"I can't get it open, any ideas?" he asked.

The other three looked around but offered nothing useful. Max stopped and considered something, then ran off to the nearest pump. He pulled out the nozzle and squeezed the trigger. A small amount of fuel, no more than a mouthful dripped out onto the concrete floor.

Steve ran up to the booth, stopping next to Zack, his breathing was so heavy he couldn't speak for a while. The zombies were now over halfway down the short gradient and probably just thirty seconds from the pumps.

Zack looked around the booth for any levers or switches that might help. After rummaging around he quickly gave up.

"That isn't going to work, you need to get the guy in the booth to authorise the fuel and we can't do that because the place is locked up," he said.

"Hang on, can't you pay by card?" asked Laura.

Tony ran over to the next pump and pulled a card out of his wallet, sliding it into the machine's control pad.

"Yeah, she's right, we can buy the fuel on a card and it will self authorise!"

The first of the zombies was now just feet away from the forecourt of the petrol station. With a clunk the pump started up and petrol flowed from it. He pointed the nozzle in the direction of the approaching zombies and continued to pump fuel at them.

Steve, Zack and Laura moved back towards the booth, keeping well away from the petrol and the fumes emanating from it. The last of the zombies seemed to have moved down from the higher ground and continued down towards them. From what they could guess there were at least sixty, maybe seventy zombies on their way and over half were now in the petrol station and moving towards Tony on the pump. With a clunk another pump burst into life as Max's credit card was finally accepted. He added more fuel to the ground and also threw it around to reach as far from the pump as possible. The first zombie was almost on him when Zack ran over and dragged him away.

"Come on man, we still need to burn the place!" shouted Zack.

As the two retreated from the pumps Tony heard them shouting and dropped his nozzle, running back to join them. All five were now stepping away from the station. Tony flipped out his lighter and ignited it, looking to Zack and Max.

"Ready?" he asked as he prepared to throw it.

"Wait!" said Zack as he grabbed his arm, "we need them all."

The group stood in silence, watching the zombie horde move through the petrol station towards them. As the final zombie stepped onto the forecourt Zack gave the nod. With one big motion Tony cast the lighter through the air and to the closest spill of fuel. At first nothing happened then there was a flash and the flames spread through the entire station. The heat was immense and forced the group back and away from the carnage.

"Come on!" shouted Zack, "Get to The Mall!"

They ran around the burning petrol station, staying on the road and at a safe distance. It appeared the inferno had done its job as there were no zombies on the road or out in the open. Laura stopped, open mouthed as she looked at the blaze. Tony turned to check what it was that had caught her eye. From the blaze half a dozen of the zombies were staggering back out and towards them. They were burning from head to toe, looking like some kind of macabre walking torch. As the flames took hold each of them slowed and then finally collapsed to the ground, the fire consuming their flesh.

Steve pushed Laura and they continued on their way towards The Mall. Without pausing they moved past the crashed bus and noted the lack of zombies near it. In just seconds they were off the road and running through the empty car park towards the main glass entrance. Zack, being taller and faster moved to the front of the group and reached the entrance first. The security shutters were up but the doors appeared locked. He banged his fists on the thick glass but to no avail. Zack arrived and the others were not far behind him.

With several low thuds a series of explosions blasted from the petrol station. The group all turned to see clouds of smoke shooting up from the burning station.

"Must be the underground petrol tanks or maybe camping gas containers," said Steve.

They stood silent, just watching the burning structure. A wail almost like the howl of wind came from the direction of the burning petrol station. A silent Tony extended his arm, pointing off into the distance. Zack and Laura looked in the direction of his hand, quickly spotting the horde.

"Oh shit!" shouted Zack.

Steve started pacing back and forth as he spotted the large mass of zombies making their way past the burning petrol station. More noise came, it was evident that there were still plenty of zombies out there.

"Why are they still coming this way?" asked Laura, her voice almost sounding hysterical.

With a swish the doors behind them swung open and a man in full riot armour stepped out. He slipped up the visor on his helmet.

"They're coming because you just lit the biggest damned beacon in the county!" he said in a grumpy voice.

Max staggered backwards, surprised by the sound. The rest just stood there in silence, watching the man in his rough and obviously well used armour. A teenager ran past him and up to Zack.

"Tim?" shouted Zack.

The excited kid slapped his hand down on Zack's, grinning with excitement.

"I got here before you, this copper found me. He's been here for more than a day, it's fucking awesome in there!" he said.

The policeman stepped forward.

"I suggest you get inside. Most of The Mall is now locked and I've prepared safe rooms, weapons and supplies. There are a few other survivors here as well, hopefully more will make it. You'll be ok for now," he said.

The group were still silent, shocked by the arrival of the policeman and then Tim. The noise of the first of the approaching zombies soon woke them up. Max was first to make a decision and stepped through the doors, he turned his head, shouting at the rest as he entered.

"Come on, we need to get ready," he said.

Zack followed with Laura, Tony and finally Steve joining them. With them all inside the main foyer the policeman stepped inside and hit a button. The thick glass doors slid shut. He placed a key into a lock and with a grinding sound a series of heavy metal shutters started lowering themselves.

The policeman removed his helmet and turned to the group.

"I take it you've seen the news? This outbreak has turned into a worldwide epidemic," he said.

"Yeah, we saw the news earlier," replied Max.

"Well, it's just got a lot worse. The military is fighting a losing battle and it's up to people like us to find a way to keep alive. Tim said you've got a lot of experience with survival manuals and strategy with things like this!" he stated in a questioning tone whilst looking at Max and Zack.

The two nodded in acknowledgement.

The policeman pointed over to a table with paperwork and equipment on it. Zack and Max walked over to it. There were detailed drawings of the retail park and shopping mall. Next to the paperwork were pile of blades, fire axes and heavy clothing. After giving the paperwork and equipment a cursory look Zack turned to face the rest of the group. At the front stood the policeman, behind him were the rest of them including Tim.

They looked at the two of them, waiting for something... anything. The policeman gave Zack a nod. With a deep breath he began.

"Okay, I've got a great idea."

Lightning Source UK Ltd.
Milton Keynes UK
UKOW040420270613

212877UK00001B/232/P